# The Crossing

The Crossing

# The Crossing

## The Chronicles Of Micki O'Sullivan
## Book 1

**_Jo Wilde_**

*I'd like to dedicate this to my family, for they have been there for me through thick and thin. Without their support, I would not be where I am today.*

*Thanks, Crazy!*

*I had my whole world ahead of me. Eager to take the plunge that life offered. Though nothing prepared me for this terrifying moment that changed everything forever. No one can save me now.*

*Not even Superman.*

# Contents

# Exodus

October swooped in, bringing an unexpected chill. The kind of chill that hot chocolate couldn't soothe. With autumn fast approaching, the weather had taken a vicious turn for the worse. The scent of snow clung heavily to the air, burning my lungs.

New York winters arrived early.

Snowflakes dotted my black coat as I entered JFK airport. I paused a minute, taking in the trillion people swarming like bees, all rushing to find their flight.

After standing in a mile-long line, I clenched my boarding pass in hand and ventured onto the plane, departing for Shreveport, Louisiana, where my dad, Henry, awaited my arrival. He lived only a few miles east in a small town called Eastwick. Population, a little more than five thousand.

I whipped out a puff of air, feeling the pressure of regret. I missed New York already. I knew nothing else. For seventeen years, my whole world centered around the Big Apple. But now, I, Micki Lea

O'Sullivan, was forced to abandon my precious home for good.

I stopped at row 13A and paused. In the chair next to mine sat a man large enough to fill two seats. A little bothered, I squeezed past him. I settled in my spot, laying my purse by my feet, and nodded to my new neighbor. I quietly blew out a long breath to calm my pounding heart. I needed a distraction. I eyed the small window and slid the shade up and gazed out. By now, the white flakes cluttered the bruised sky. A slight breeze tousled the snow this way and that.

My mind drifted to a luggage handler across the tarmac. The man hurled one bag after another over the rail and down into the bin, several feet below. I gave in to a curt giggle. Several pieces of baggage had missed the container and laid in broken pieces on the ground. Clothing of rainbow colors scurried in the wind to and fro as if in a cat and mouse chase. The handler appeared clueless as he continued in a rhythmic beat.

Restless, I sat back in my seat and started to close my eyes, but not before I checked my seatbelt once more. My hands shook as my heart remained lodged in my throat. First time to fly and first-time jitters too. I listened to the gentle thrum of the engine idling. But my agitation got the best of me.

The man next to me, bathed in British Sterling, agitated me to no end. The left side of his body spilled over onto my seat, pressing me against the window. I started to speak up, but I decided to keep quiet. Ending up handcuffed by a police officer and missing my flight sounded like a bad idea. A recent scuffle with the law taught me a valuable lesson. Jail and stale baloney sandwiches sucked.

I glanced up and met two small hazel eyes. A little boy no more than three, peeked over his seat, flashing a shy smile. I teased the toddler poking my tongue at him, and he shyly responded with a giggle ducking behind his mother.

Moments later, his happy mood morphed into a squalling temper tantrum. I reached inside my handbag and dug out my earbuds and cell phone. I swore under my breath that I would never have children. I jammed the buds in my ears and slumped down into my seat, listening to *The Chainsmokers*. Maybe music would settle my nerves. Crammed together with total strangers, reminded me of a sardine can. I preferred riding in a taxi with a backseat full of drunks. At least they made me laugh and only rode for a short duration.

All at once, the engine revved with mounting power. A loud ding drew the passenger's attention to a flickering green sign that hung on a panel above the seated guest. Time to buckle up for takeoff. A rush of clicks stirred the coach, and a burst of energy spread throughout. I hurried to check my seatbelt again and then grabbed the armrest, eyes shut tight, embracing for an anticipated takeoff.

The man next to me, up to his elbows, was buried in his paperwork. Documents scattered across the small folding table that hovered barely above his thick lap. A frequent flyer, my guess and not a worry in the world if this flight crashed.

People began to stir as I caught the attendants ushering toward the front, grabbing their seats, and hunkering down as the wheels commenced churning and gaining momentum.

As the powerful jet sped down the runway, anxiety punched me in the gut. I listened to the drum of the wheels gobbling up the pavement, and then my stomach somersaulted as we lifted into the gray sky. My skin paled to white chalk, making me regret not taking a Trailways bus. I shut my eyes tight, squeezing the armrest.

After a terrifying thirty-five seconds, the plane straightened its nose, and the quiet hum of the engine eased my fear. I inhaled a deep breath and smiled. "Whew! That wasn't so bad," I mumbled to myself.

I peeked under my lashes at the man beside me. A slow rise and fall enfolded his chest. His gray head tilted to the right, hanging into the aisle. He had fallen asleep. My brows bunched together, baffled at how anyone slept through takeoff?

Just when I started to relax, I glanced out the tiny window, and my stomach dropped. Nothing but tiny green and brown square patches blanketed the land. "Geez!" I muttered under my breath and slammed the small shade down. I sat back, clenching my chest. It baffled me how a mere man was capable of creating something made mostly of metal that was capable of soaring above the clouds. My first time to fly and absolutely my last.

The coach had quieted, and even the little boy sitting up front had fallen asleep in his mother's lap. I leaned back in my seat and stretched out the kink in my neck and then closed my eyes. My mind drifted over the past few weeks and the legal troubles that had gotten me into this mess.

Though I remembered a time when life was much simpler. Before my parents divorced, living in Hell's Kitchen on 51st street in New York City was like my little pie in the sky. Congested traffic, cars honking, and the busy stream of people all strolling to the same relentless beat. The smell of pin oak and ice skating in Central Park during Christmas, hot dogs, and exhaust fumes was my little piece of heaven. It was my escape from my parents' fighting.

Every morning, I'd take a brisk walk to the *Coffee Pot*, grabbing a toasty bagel and a hot Cappuccino before catching the school bus.

Henry drove a taxi. Joan, my mom, worked for a prestigious couple, Phil and Anna Montgomery, who lived on the Upper East Side of Manhattan. Joan was an assistant, the go-to girl. The couple recently gave birth to a boy. Mrs. Montgomery needed someone to run errands. Joan couldn't have found a job more suitable for her. She had a knack for shopping for bargains and made quite an impression on Mr. Montgomery.

Though my family lived from paycheck to paycheck, we had all we needed. A roof over our heads and food to eat. For a little spending money, after school and on weekends, I worked a part-time job walking dogs. The money came in handy if I wanted to catch a movie or go ice skating.

I didn't care about hanging out with kids from school. I wore the badge socially inept across my chest proudly. Besides, making friends had its downside.

Boys often asked me out, but considering their lack of probity, I declined their offer. They didn't see me. They only saw my outer beauty, hair of honey, long cascading curls, blue eyes, and curves. The girls hated me despite how hard I tried to hide in the shadows.

I supposed it turned out for the best. I had a secret. One I didn't share with anyone. As far back as I could remember, I possessed a gift. Not even my parents knew. Since the age of five, I saw auras. Various shades of green to bright red. Each color revealed the truth about the individual and at times, their deepest darkest secrets. My colorful auras never steered me wrong. Not once.

Alone all the time, I found ways to stay busy… *the theater*. A diehard passion of mine. Henry and I jumped at any opportunity to see a Broadway play. The Phantom of the Opera sat top of the list of our favorites. We both teared up many times. A young soprano becomes the obsession of a disfigured musical genius who lives beneath the Paris *Opéra* House.

Joan, my mom, didn't share the passion. It became mine and Henry's special event.

Then our whole world changed when Joan went to work for a corporate company. Mr. Montgomery offered her a position at his law firm. Apart from my mom's attractive features, glistening, chestnut hair, tall, and hour-glass curves, Joan didn't have any specific skills for the corporate world. A pencil pusher or fetch the coffee described her qualifications best.

I think for the first time in her life, she found an opportunity. A job with promise. Even I understood her newfound zest. As a young woman, she had missed out on so much. Joan and Henry were high school sweethearts. He was seventeen, and Joan was only sixteen when she got pregnant with me.

When their families heard the happy announcement, it was a huge disappointment. Both families had big plans for their children. Getting pregnant was not one of them. After a couple of months passed, Henry's family, the O'Sullivans, and Joan's family, the Watsons, planned a small wedding. In the beginning, Henry and Joan, deeply in love, were confident they had gotten their happily ever after.

Then the happily-ever-after ceased, and Joan gave birth to a baby girl… *me*. My entrance into this world wreaked havoc for the two star-crossed lovers.

Soon, Henry and Joan came to understand the late-night bottle feeding and changing diapers were only the beginning of parenthood. It was tough for them. Growing up and facing a heavy responsibility wasn't as easy as they once thought.

The couple settled into their roles, but it was not smooth sailing. My parents fought a lot. Every week, they had at least one good argument. It usually ended when Henry ducked out the front door when Joan started slinging dishes. I hung out in my room until the house quieted.

The happiness between Henry and Joan never completed a full circle. Tension rose in the house as angry silence loomed.

Then the day came when my world shattered into a million pieces. Joan left Henry. I saw it coming, but I turned the other cheek, pretending their arguments were typical.

The affair ripped our family in two and set Henry into a spiraling depression. Unable to grasp the fact that his seventeen-year marriage was finished, the reality crushed him. I saw it in his eyes, his walk, his slumped shoulders.

Joan, aloof to the hurt she caused, moved out and into a penthouse with all the expensive perks of the Upper East Side of Manhattan, compliments of her wealthy boss, Phil Montgomery.

In the divorce, Henry got our home, and Joan got me. I think she thought giving Henry the house would atone for her infidelity. And then again, the sky was the limit, marrying her loaded fiancé. Where money was concerned, Joan had the world at her feet.

Henry received a business offer from an out-of-towner that he couldn't refuse. So, he sold the house and moved to Eastwick, Louisiana, where he settled down in a quiet country community. The new surroundings gave Henry the perfect escape. I think watching his wife with a wealthy and powerful attorney was like a swift kick in the gut, more than he could bear.

As our lives shifted, we had to learn a new balance. When Grandma Martha O'Sullivan died, Grandpa Brín moved in with Henry. It was bittersweet. It really crushed Grandpa losing his partner of almost fifty years. Moving in with Henry helped to ease the loneliness. It comforted both men. Every Sunday, the two went fishing down at the bayou. They both loved the outdoors and fishing was at the top of the list. Maybe Grandpa's second. He seemed to be quite social with the widows of Eastwick.

As for the divorce, it was Henry's unexpected break. Henry took the money from the house sale and partnered up with a renowned Eastwick business partner and started his construction business. Carpentry was in Henry's blood. Grandpa was a carpenter in his younger days, and his father before him and so on down the line. The trade ran deep in the O'Sullivan family and was referred to as an art rather than a trade. Henry was brilliant, and his talents paid off.

Living more than a thousand miles apart, I only got to see Henry and Grandpa on holidays and summers. It was a welcome visit and an exhausting return back to living with Joan and my stepfather, Phil. I didn't get along with him. He didn't have the patience for children. He rarely saw his own son. And a teenager intensified his intolerance to almost a breaking point, and it wasn't a lack of trying on my part. I loathed my stepfather.

Phil stayed busy a lot with his firm. He needed absolute quiet in the house at all times. Having a noisy teenager blasting heavy metal at all hours of the night hit his rage button. He'd go into meltdown at least twice a week. I liked pushing his buttons. And he had many.

Appearances weighed heavily on Phil's shoulders. At all times, he demanded we wear our expensive apparel by some stupid designer with a name no one could pronounce. I defied his demands by paying homage to vintage fashion with a modern, sassy twist, all black. I wore nothing but. I wanted my clothes to reflect my dislike for his brainfart rules. Plus, an added bonus... *pissing Phil off*. All the more reason to black-punk up.

As my spidey senses warned me, after a few months into their marriage, Joan's glee began to wane. Though, shopping helped to ease her woes until Phil put his foot down, demanding a strict budget and firing Joan at the firm. My mom stayed furious for weeks. She loved her position at the firm. I didn't understand how she could be around Phil twenty-four-seven. He was such a nasty sort. But okay. Whatever floated her boat. Happy Joan was much easier to live with. Phil failed to get the memo.

Then my life began to improve when I got busted with a couple of blunts in my possession. I tried to defend myself. "I swear, it's not mine!" I declared vehemently. Neither Joan nor Phil fell for that excuse, and even Henry and Grandpa questioned my defense. Displeasing Phil or Joan didn't bother me, but disappointing Henry ripped through me. I hated having to look him in the face after I'd disappointed him.

Joan and Phil were at their wits' end, and lucky me got sent to live with Henry. This was the best punishment ever. I never wanted to live with Joan. I preferred staying with my dad. As I predicted, Joan packed my bags, sending me straight to Henry.

Phil stood with a wide grin plastered on his face, waving goodbye as I boarded the plane. His intent wasn't to wish me a happy bon voyage. He was there to make sure I didn't miss my flight. He hated me. That was one thing we both agree on. There was no love between us.

Ostentation clung to Phil like dermatitis. With his fancy law firm and his silver chrome Jaguar and his fortress-tight mansion, Phil was a pompous man with a large cork up his butt. His bowlegged walk confirmed my suspicions.

* * *

My flight arrived on time at noon. I took the first flight departing New York. Phil couldn't get rid of me fast enough. I disembarked the plane, lugging my large suitcase on wheels as every scent imaginable struck my nostrils. From bubble gum to cigarettes. I could count on my allergies acting up tonight. Henry would need to stop at a pharmacy on our way home. Of course, Louisiana loved taunting my allergies. The crepe myrtle perfumed the air, making my sneezing run amok, and then the constant rain added to my flare-ups.

I spotted Henry right off, waiting for me at gate 10. He was sorta hard to miss. A tall figure clad in faded blue jean overalls stood at a full six-three toting a frown the size of the Grand Canyon.

Judging by his drawn expression, my fate was sealed. Grounded for eternity. Though Henry reminded me of a gentle bear, he didn't play. Whenever I wound up in trouble, he ruled with a firm hand.

Lugging my suitcase on wheels and with my backpack strapped to my shoulders, I padded my way to Henry. When I reached his side, he drew me into his warm arms and hugged me tightly. Then he pulled me from his chest at arm's length and eyed me like I was five years old again and had fallen off my tricyle. "You've grown a foot, Mick." His deep, blue eyes gleamed. "You wanna grab a burger?"

I got the feeling that Henry was a little nervous.

I ran my eyes over the throng of people. "Hey, where's Grandpa?"

"Pop stayed home. He had some work to do."

I giggled. "Knitting again?" Grandpa had a stroke a year ago, and ever since he'd been... *different.*

"Yep. But don't tell anyone. It's a man's thing." Henry bounced a short shrug.

"I hope he's not knitting me another sweater."

"Oh, yeah! That one with one sleeve that hung to the floor," Henry chuckled.

"Remember Grandpa swore it was all the rage?"

"How could I forget. Pop planned to sell millions."

"Yeah, one of my more unforgettable moments. I still have the emotional scars from wearing it to school. The relentless teases went on for months." I frowned, but inside I was laughing.

"Jellybean, hate to tell you, but we parents and grandparents are meant to ruin our kids' lives," Henry winked. "So, are you hungry? A good excuse not to eat Grandpa's cooking tonight."

I rolled my eyes. "Good idea!" Then my face grew solemn. "Dad, I know I'm grounded. We don't need to do the talk," I paused. "Just give me my sentencing, please." Disrespect wasn't my intention. If I told the whole truth, I doubted he'd believe me.

"Yes, you certainly are grounded, young lady." He blew out a sharp sigh, rocking on his heels. "Even under the harshest punishments, one still needs to eat."

"All right. I guess I can eat." A slight scowl creased between my brows.

Henry was a handsome man. He didn't look old enough to be a parent of a seventeen-year-old. Tall and athletic, light brown hair, and a smile that could light up a whole room. His kind eyes always put me at ease. I was lucky to have him for my dad.

"Good!" Henry smiled, taking my suitcase.

We ended up at MOOYAH Burgers and Fries downtown. My favorite place in this backward little town of Eastwick. There was nothing better than sinking my teeth into a white, sugary beignet, except for the burgers here in Louisiana. They were mind-blowing.

After the server took our order, Dad began his speech. I drowned myself in a chocolate shake while he preached about the downfalls of using drugs. Jesus! It was only two joints.

"Your mother and I might not be together, but we both are equally responsible for raising you." He inhaled a deep breath of patience and then continued. "What were you thinking? You got arrested for possession of marijuana with the intent to distribute?"

"Yes, Dad, I know. I was there." I fiddled with my straw averting my eyes to the floor.

Sadness rolled off Henry's shoulders. "If it hadn't been for Phil, you would've been charged as an adult. Your whole future would've gone down the pipes." Henry's words struck me like bullets.

"Well, the charges were dropped, and I don't anticipate any more problems."

"You have one year left before college. Don't make any plans other than school." Henry's firm voice left me with no doubt about my bleak future. No fun until I turned forty-five.

"I get it. No life." I slid down into my chair and crossed my arms. "Dad, those days are behind me. I swear! No more pot!"

"From now on, you're walking a fine line until graduation. Do I make myself clear?"

"Yes sir," I replied, crosser than I intended.

Dad's tight expression relaxed into a stern but gentle smile. "I get that it hasn't been easy since your mom and I split. But it doesn't mean we love you any less. Sometimes adults grow apart."

"You and Mother didn't grow apart." My brows collided. "Mother dumped you for a rich douche bag." The second the words came out of my mouth, I regretted it.

Henry's smile flipped upside down. "Thanks for reminding me." That axed our conversation and made our meal rigid and quiet. I didn't know what had gotten into me. Henry didn't cause the affair. Joan made that decision all on her own. Still, I bet he blamed himself.

"Dad, I'm sorry. These days I don't even know myself."

A loving curve touched his mouth. "That makes two of us, but we're going to pull through."

I nodded, half-smiling into my burger.

When we arrived home, Grandpa appeared from his man cave, the basement. He did all his tinkering and sleep there. "Well, if it isn't my outlaw, grand-daughter." He scooped me up into a tight hug. Grandpa loved Snickers ice cream a bit too much and revealed his indulgence by his broad waist. He'd make a perfect Santa with his white beard and rosy cheeks.

My eyes sparkled. "Grandpa, I'm a reformed outlaw. I learned my lesson." I leaned into the nook of his arm and hugged his portly waist.

Grandpa came to America when he was a young man, and to this day, he still fostered a strong Irish accent. "Glad your home where you belong, Lassie. We need someone to dig for worms when your da and I go fishin'."

"Uh... I am not digging up worms or cleaning foul fish," I cringed. "I don't even eat fish."

Henry and Grandpa burst into chortles.

15

"Off you go then. Go look at your room. Your da has been really workin' hard." Grandpa encouraged.

My eyes appled. "Really?" Excitement tickled my heart. I darted straight up the stairs to the attic. Dad bought this creepy one-hundred-year-old Victorian house, including creaks and cobwebs and none of the modern conveniences. Although Henry promised me a fully functioning bathroom. I didn't hold my breath. He'd been working on renovations since he bought the house three years ago. The house needed weather insulation. Cold and drafty in the winter and insufferably hot in the summer. Glad I had only my senior year to finish.

I hadn't decided which college I wanted to attend. It depended on my grades and the deepest pocket for my tuition. Art was my only interest. Maybe after I earned my bachelor's degree, I might teach.

I trudged up two flights of stairs and off to the side, then I climbed another flight, leading directly to the attic. When I reached my door, I turned the squeaky knob and entered. I expected the usual plank floors and twin bed, but when I lifted my eyes, I stood speechless. The old attic had been wholly transformed, including a new bathroom.

Henry leaned over my shoulder and said. "I thought I'd surprise you with a welcome-home gift." Joy bubbled in his eyes.

"Dad, it's great!" I twirled on my toes and hugged him. The room was beyond my wildest dreams. More work was needed, but with a new queen-sized bed, dresser, and nightstand to match and a drafting ta-

16

ble for my artwork, it was a promising start. I loved this old attic. The square footage was the size of the second floor, like a loft. I noted that the vaulted ceiling now had a new skylight directly above my bed. Great for stargazing. At the very back, the center wall had a circular stain-glass window that embellished the room with bright colors of pink and blue. On the other two walls, there were several small windows, opening the attic to loads of sunlight and fresh air. I spotted a 52-inch television, and some CDs nicely stacked on the shelf on the other side of my dresser.

I padded over to the dresser and picked up one of the CDs. I lifted my gaze to Henry, "Casablanca, starring Humphrey Bogart and Ingrid Bergman." I cradled the CD to my chest. "You remember how much I love black and white films. Thanks, Dad."

"You're welcome." He scratched his bristled chin. "It's not much, but you can add your own touch. You know, paint the walls. Do whatever you like," he smiled, eyeing the ample space."

My eyes glided over the room once more. "Dad, it's the best!" I grinned. "This is perfect."

"I'm glad you like it, jellybean. Since you're going to be living here and let's not forget that you're grounded, I thought your bedroom could use some sprucing up."

Then my smile morphed into a brick. For a minute, I'd forgotten about my awaiting doom.

# Eastwick High

On the first day of school, I woke up to the aroma of sizzling bacon and coffee. Grandpa was up early, stirring in the kitchen preparing breakfast, including a sack lunch. One tasty peanut butter sandwich accompanied by Cheetos. And for dessert, he threw in a honey bun. Though not my favorite, still to me, it was a special meal that only my grandpa could make.

Henry and I rolled up to Eastwick High and quickly found a parking space. My heart pounded with first-day jitters. As we slipped out of the truck, I took a deep whiff of the lingering honeysuckle that drifted in the air. It was better than any of Mom's expensive perfumes. Yet my allergies disagreed. I held back a sneeze.

As we approached the main entrance, I quickly sized up the place like any other small-town school. It covered all the basics but nothing extraordinary. No grandiose red-carpet air. Only two buildings. The elementary was on the west side, and the high school was on the complete opposite, east side. I think the other grades were in the middle.

Henry accompanied me to the office. I tried talking him into letting me register on my own, but he insisted on escorting me as if I were a five-year-old. Yet, taking me to school must've meant something special to him. Henry never took time off work. His job sorta overran him.

When we entered the office, two jocks tapped the windowpane flirting with me from the hallway, giggling like they'd lost their brain cells. No question, those two boys planned to alert every other male about the new girl. Meaning *me*.

I preferred being the daisy on the wall. I stood out far too much for my comfort. I tried playing my looks down by avoiding make-up. It really didn't help. I still got whistled at and eyed like I was a piece of candy.

Once we finished registering, Dad rushed off to work, and I headed to my first class, calculus.

As the day ventured onward, I managed to survive the whispers, soft giggles, and the constant stares. Five more classes to go. I blew out a barb-wired sigh. My terrible first day would end, and tomorrow would bring forth another day like this.

Unloading my math book and gathering books for round two, I almost bumped into three girls looming by my locker. All three were in a deadlock stare at me. The dark-haired girl spoke first. "I'm Wendy Belle. We have calculus together," she smiled and paused, facing her two friends. "This is Cindy Ward and Ella James."

My eyes bounced between the three faces as I replied, "Hello." I shut my locker with a muffled clank and turned to face the girls. Wendy, the one who did the introductory, I judged as the alpha. Flawless porcelain skin, too bright against her contrasting shoulder-length, raven hair, and a little on the thin side. Eh, attractive, I supposed. She stood almost as tall as me, and strangely, I couldn't see her aura.

The other two girls' auras faded under the fluorescent lighting as if they were a hologram. Weird, I thought. Cindy stood about 5'1 and had acne and frizzy, mousy hair. Not a pretty brown at all. Ella had fiery red hair and more freckles than I cared to count. In fact, her freckles made her face look disfigured, and her blue eyes were dull and lifeless. The way she slumped her shoulders, avoiding eye contact and appearing skittish, made me wonder if she might be a druggie.

The girl, Wendy, jarred my attention. "You should sit with us at lunch." Her smile brightened her hazel eyes.

"Uh… sure! I'll look you up." I halfheartedly shrugged, accepting their offer, not wishing to piss these girls off on my first day. Who knew? Maybe my luck had changed making new friends.

When Joan got custody of me, I had to leave everything I knew at Hell's Kitchen. When I transferred to a private school, Manhattan High for Girls, I didn't bother making friends. The students were all rich snobs. I didn't mesh well with most and was often singled out. Their relentless teasing was a wide range of name bashing, calling me nothing short of a hooker. The bullying went past the teacher's notice. Most of the kids' parents paid hefty donations. I think the school didn't want to challenge their most significant contributors.

Funny though, the very girls that slandered my good name were sexually active, *unlike me*. I was a virgin in every sense of the word. Not even a kiss. As lame as it sounded, I wanted to find a boy I liked first. That was like finding gold at the end of a rainbow. It didn't happen. I towered over most boys. At five-ten, it was hard finding a boy my height.

"Wonderful!" Wendy almost jumped for joy like she'd won the Nobel Prize. "We'll see you at lunch." Her eagerness set my teeth on edge. Then again, I assumed this town rarely fostered new students. Glad someone made the initiative. No one else had gone to the trouble. I couldn't blame them. Apart from my height, wearing a nose ring, and black attire, I appeared intimidating.

"Cool." I sounded a bit stiff. "I'll see you then." I watched as all three girls flashed broad smiles and scooted off down the hall, fading into the throng of students.

Social Studies was next, room 222. I sprinted, knowing the class was on the far north side. I pushed past the double doors when I collided with a boy who seemed to have popped out of nowhere. My books went flying along with my feet. I gracefully landed on my back, sprawled out on the sidewalk. "Ow!" I mumbled, adding a few curse words.

"I'm sorry." A male's deep voice pierced my ears. "Are you okay?" His soothing tone probed further. "Let me help you up." He offered his hand to mine with a smile.

I cuffed my hand over my eyes. The boy's outline was dark and towering against the sunlight. "Uh... okay." I sounded like my brain had taken a vacation. I took his hand, and he lifted me back to my feet as I stumbled into his embrace. The second our eyes locked, my breath stalled. I stared into two violet eyes and a dimpled smile bright enough to melt the North Pole. His hands rested on my hips for a moment.

I couldn't pull my eyes away. The boy was stunning like he'd been airbrushed, corn-silk hair that kissed the blue sky and his muscular arms, bare, strutting a tat on his upper right arm. A Celtic symbol. I remembered learning about this in Humanities.

"Are you hurt?" The boy asked as his eyes roamed over me.

"No, I'm fine. Sorry for..."

He interrupted. "No problem. These are yours, I believe." He held out two thick books.

I took them, hiding my eyes under my lashes. "Uh... thank you."

"Well, I'll see you around." His smile was strikingly white against his tanned face.

"Yeah, see you," I mumbled, unable to peel my eyes from his angelic face.

Then he broke the enchantment, disappearing inside the building. The last bell rang, and I darted to class, late for Social Studies.

\* \* \*

Lunchtime rolled around as I entered the double doors to the cafeteria. My stomach growled as I peeked into my lunch bag. "Ugh!" I mumbled as my stomach roiled, staring down at a peanut butter sandwich. Sure enough, if I ate that, I'd lose my cookies. Without hesitation, I tossed my lunch in the trash and grabbed a Coke, making my way through the assemblage of students, searching for Wendy and her friends.

I spotted their heads in the back and edged my way toward them. I wasn't wholly on board with becoming bosom buddies with the trio. Usually, cliquey girls stayed in their own little bubble. No one ever penetrated their phantom boundaries either. My spidey senses made me question their motive. Then I shook off my suspicion. I shouldn't be so jaded. This wasn't New York. Besides, anyone judging me by my pretty face had another thing coming. I was more than capable of holding my own.

The dark-haired girl, Wendy, was standing up, waving her arms like she was flagging a plane down. Kinda hard to miss. I drew in a deep breath and edged my way to their table.

"Hey, come sit by me!" Wendy patted the chair next to her. The other two girls remained quiet. Such a weird trio.

I smiled with my Coke in hand and took the seat offered. "Thanks," I said.

Wendy started the conversation right off. "Are you new to Eastwick?" she drawled with a heavy dose of sugar.

"Uh, not really. My dad's been living here for the last three years." I didn't want to tell them my entire story.

The two tongue-tied girls shared a glance but didn't speak.

"Oh, your parents must be divorced," Wendy summed up. "Were you living with your mother?"

I paused, unscrewed the top off my Coke, tilted my head back and took a gulp. The fizz burned going down. "Uh...yes." I decided to give her a little bit of my personal info. Though I had no plans to share my run-in with the law.

"I hear that when the mother sends her child off to Daddy, the kid's usually knocked up, or they got into a scuffle with the authorities." Wendy laughed, but the tease was really a dig behind the smile.

"Nope. Not me," I denied, giving Wendy no ammo.

The glint in her eyes was evident that she didn't believe me. What did I care? I didn't owe her an explanation. "What's up with the gloomy garb? The nose ring and black lipstick to match?" Wendy's manicured eyebrow rose inquiringly.

My lips morphed into a scowl. "It's a trend I picked up in New York." I took another sip of my Coke. I had to give Wendy credit. She didn't relent.

Wendy went on to add, "I hope you like it here. We seldom get new people. We three have known each other since elementary." A syrupy smile tipped the corners of her mouth. "We're having a small gathering. A few friends. Why don't you come? We can pick you up?"

The other two girls nodded and flashed a sheepish smile.

"Uh, when?" I hated getting put on the spot.

"Friday night," Wendy ushered her reply.

"Tomorrow night?" I asked.

"Yes, and I won't take no for an answer." Wendy grasped my hand and nodded to the other two girls. "Don't y'all agree?"

Suddenly Ella and Cindy leaped for joy, coming out of their shell. "Yeah, it'd be so much fun!" They giggled like children at recess.

"Absolutely! We need new blood." Ella, the dumpy one, added, but Cindy must've kicked her under the table as she jolted with a sharp yap. I caught the dirty look that Ella darted at Cindy.

Wendy cut her eyes at the two girls, giving a glare of warning, and then turned her attention back to me. "It's settled. I'll pick you up on Friday, five o'clock sharp." She flashed a smile. I ignored my hesitation and decided to give her the benefit of the doubt.

"Let me clear it with my dad first." Since I was grounded, I had a perfect excuse to cancel, but my curiosity tugged at me fiercely. Meeting new people would be good, even though these three seemed to be too clingy for my taste.

"No problem. Let me give you my number." Wendy held her palm out for my cell. Hesitance washed over me, but I didn't see any way around it. I dug my phone out from my back pocket and placed it in her hand. I watched as she entered her digits in my contacts. "Here you go." She handed my phone back. "Call me tonight as soon as you find out," she flashed a pursed grin. My spidey senses chilled my skin. I didn't like the vibe this chick or her posse emitted.

I feigned a smile back. "Thanks. It sounds fun."

# A Girl's Hope

I was so happy when my feet touched the ground, exiting the bus a block from my house. There was an annoying light-skinned, black boy, tall and skinny, giving me the evil eye like I'd robbed his lunch. I blew him off, rolling my eyes. Every now and then, I'd glance in his direction and catch his ireful glint. I started to confront him, but since it was my first day and with no solid friendships established, I kept my opinion to myself.

Grandpa was at his lady friend's house, so it was Henry and me tonight. I knew when he got off work, he'd be hungry. I tapped my chin, thinking. Pizza, or a homemade meal? If I cooked a nice dinner, he might let me go Friday night. I went straight for the fridge and dug around to inspect its contents. We had frozen chicken and a couple of T-bone steaks. Steaks would defrost faster than chicken.

I pulled a hairband from my pocket and wrapped my hair into a ponytail. I grabbed the steaks and ripped the plastic cover off. I reached up in the cabinet, pulled down a rack, and laid the steaks out. A little trick Joan taught me. The steaks should be ready to cook in an hour. I gathered two large potatoes, wrapped them in foil, tossed them in the oven, and set the temperature at 400 Fahrenheit. Next, I threw a bag of frozen green beans with a slice of bacon in a pan of water and turned the burner on low and then added a teaspoon of salt.

I set the table with mismatched plates, one avocado green, and one salmon pink. The mark of a truly divorced bachelor. I stood back, eyeing the table, and nodded in approval.

I recalled when Joan assigned me to set the table. It was my favorite thing to do at dinner. I took pride in setting the flatware in its proper place and placing a bouquet of daisies with two candles on each side. Things were different then. Now Joan had servants to do the task. A stark contrast to what I grew accustomed to.

After I finished prepping everything, I sunk into the couch and started on my homework. If Henry saw how hard I was working, he may be more inclined to let me go. A girl could only hope.

When Henry walked through the door with a heavy huff, I'd just pulled out the steaks from the broiler and set them on the stove. They were perfect, medium rare, and dripping in juice. "I'm in the kitchen!" I hollered.

"My goodness!" Henry stopped at the doorframe; his blue eyes glistened with surprise. "I didn't know you knew how to cook." He watched as I pulled out the potatoes.

"Yep, go have a seat. You wanna glass of sweet tea?" I tossed over my shoulder.

"Sure!" His voice went up a note.

"Go on. Have a seat. I'll bring it to you."

Henry's face brightened. "Yes, ma'am." He stopped off in the bathroom across from his office to wash his hands and then made his way to the dining room, seating himself at the head of the table.

I joined him with two piping hot plates filled to the brim. "Dad, there's sour cream and butter for the potatoes and A-1 for your steak."

"Pass me some of that," he spoke, his mouth chewing on a bite of steak.

"Which one?"

"All of them?" he chuckled.

I laughed and handed him the condiments. As I began to slice my steak, Henry moaned. "This is the best ever!" he chewed in awe.

I snickered. "I doubt that." I took a healthy bite and shut my eyes, tasting the sweet juices of the tender T-bone. Nothing like a cut of fresh beef to sink your teeth into.

"How was your first day?" Henry inquired between bites.

"I made friends with three girls," I shrugged.

"Are they nice?"

"I guess." I took a bite of my green beans. "They invited me to meet a few of their friends." I dared not say party.

"When?" Henry's dark brow perked.

"Tomorrow night," I answered lightheartedly.

"And I'm assuming you would like to go?" The glint in his blue eyes told me that he was on to me.

"It'd be nice to make friends, but I know I'm grounded." I took a bite of my potatoes.

Dad's smile morphed into laughter. "I knew this wonderful dinner had a hitch." Then he paused, studying me. "Don't tell your mother, but how about I let you go, and we see how well you do. I want you back no later than midnight."

My mouth formed into an O. "You're kidding? I can go?"

Dad hesitated. "Let's call this a clean slate. But one slip up, and you're grounded forever!" Henry was not budging on that rule, and it was more than fair.

"Sweet! I promise, Dad. I won't let you down." I reached over and kissed him on the cheek.

"Do your homework, and I'll wash the dishes," Henry offered.

"Done and done. I only have these two plates to wash, and my homework's finished."

# Strange Bedfellows

For an early fall, nature graced us with unusually warm weather, even for Louisiana.

Over an hour, trapped in Ella's car, an old Volkswagen beetle, I listened to Wendy and her duo, Cindy and Ella, argue about the proper etiquette of wearing white. I brought this on myself. I picked these three gals. I rolled my eyes as I looked out my side window.

Reaching North Beach, we climbed out of the car in time to see the sun slip behind an endless stretch of blue-green water. I paused for a brief moment taking in the contrasting blue sky against the golden orange and inhaled the fresh salty air. I liked this place already.

I followed the girls down to the beach. Seagulls chirped afar along with the steady sound of the tide crashing against the shore, winding tiny streams of water onto the white crystal sand.

This beach was much different than the murky coastline in New York. I wished we had come earlier. More daylight to bask in its beauty.

Eager to feel the cool white sand between my toes, I took my tennis shoes off and dug my feet into the tiny grains. I quietly moaned. I could live here forever.

A gentle breeze tousled my hair as I joined Wendy and the other two girls making their way toward a blazing fire not far ahead on the beachfront. I spotted three heads hovering around the campfire. That must be our destination.

I just remembered that I needed to call Henry and check-in. I patted my pockets and quickly discovered I'd left my phone sitting on my nightstand. Crap! Henry was going to be furious.

One problem at a time. First, I needed to survive the night with Wendy and those hair-brained girls. I might not know them very well, but I knew enough to know they were weird. Ella and Cindy never uttered a word without Wendy's permission. Talk about strange.

I'd become a cynic at my young age of seventeen. Where I came from, if you got caught strolling the streets with your head in the clouds, it guaranteed a mugging.

As we drew closer to the fire, three heads came into focus, and dread sunk my stomach. Clad in black leather vests and tattoo-covered arms, three males, that I assumed were bikers, hovered around the fire, laughing and drinking beer. I'd hoped the three Harleys glistening in the dusk back at the parking area belonged to another party. Though not another breathing soul was in sight.

Then one of the bikers stepped into the light, digging a drink out of the ice chest, and I gaped. It was the cute boy from school. Though we hadn't officially met, my face flushed with embarrassment. I bit my bottom lip, watching his muscled arm flex as he pulled out a beer.

I hoped he didn't remember me. How mortifying would that be? On my first day of school, my eyes were glued to the schedule when I collided into him, landing flat on my rump. I imagined how I must've looked to him peeking out from under a blonde mop of hair. Not cool at all.

My curiosity about the boy spiked. At least a head taller than the other two, his golden hair gleamed like honey in the glow of the fire. His eyes suddenly caught mine, and I quickly averted my eyes and heated cheeks.

"Hey! Wanna beer?" Wendy jarred me from my thoughts.

I wrinkled my nose. "You got anything else?" I might look like a party girl dressed in leather and lace, but I never cared for alcohol.

"C'mon! Join the fun. Don't be shy." Wendy grabbed my hand and led me closer to the fire and offered a dump-yard-worthy lawn chair with a missing ribbon. I sat in the chair, feeling like the center dish at the dinner table. "I'll be back in a flash with that Coke."

"Okay." I shrugged uneasily.

Wendy disappeared for a few minutes and returned with an ice-cold Coke in hand. "Here you go." A smile rested on her face, but a sense of disquiet twisted my stomach. "Have fun!" She waved to me as she and her posse faded into the twilight, leaving me alone.

"Wait!" I twisted in my chair, searching for them. "Where are you going?" I shouted, but Wendy and the girls had already slipped away. I blinked back shock. Surely, they didn't leave me stranded.

Soon darkness swallowed the sunset, and I sat wringing my hands. Music stirred the sea breeze as a favorite song of mine played, *I Warned Myself by Charlie Puth.* The song seemed a bit ironic. My spidey senses cautioned me about those three girls. If Wendy left, I faced walking a good sixty miles home.

I watched as the three bikers huddled in a tight circle, whispering among themselves and cutting their eyes back at me. Judging by their glower, I got the impression they disliked my company.

A shadow caught my eye as I spotted one of the bikers sauntering his way toward me, carting a seedy grin and a dark, ruby-red bottle clenched in his hand. I noted that the boy hung back with the other biker. His face was contorted with anger, scowling at me.

When the man reached my side, he planted himself down on the sand facing me, a cigarette, burnt to the butt, clung to his bottom lip, along with an odor of sweat and beer. I leaned away, trying not to cringe.

"Bonjour!" he drawled in a deep throaty French. I recognized his accent. The usual Cajun French in these parts. But he didn't have to utter a word for me to decide if I liked him. His long inky hair knotted in tangles and his ragged jeans speckled with grime gave me reason enough not to care for his company. Judging by his sharp chiseled face, he had a couple of years on everyone else.

"Why so gloomy?" he asked.

I eyed him with suspicion. "I'm not sad."

"Your frown stretches as long as the beach," he teased. "Allow me to introduce myself and company. I am Diablo, and that fine trappin' man by the fire is my long-time friend, Romeo. Forget the pouty kid sitting on the beer chest. We're friends of Wendy's." He flipped his cigarette off to the side and blew a stream of gray smoke from his thin lips. "And you are?"

I paused, taking in a good look at his old friend, Romeo. He looked just as dirty and sketchy as Diablo. "Micki O'Sullivan," I answered and then rushed to ask, "Where is Wendy?" I craned my neck. A spurt of hope shot through me.

The Cajun didn't reply. He preferred roaming his lustful eyes over my body like he was photographing me for some dirty hobby later. I tightened my thin shawl over my shoulders. "Don't worry, babee. I have plenty of wine. Oui?" he offered, holding up the same ruby-jeweled bottle he continued to grip tight to his hairy chest.

I inspected the strange liquid. Its consistency reminded me of syrup, too thick for wine. A sudden compulsion rooted through me. "Uh… thanks, but no thanks. I have a drink." I kept an eye of caution between the Cajun and me. "I need to get home. Where is Wendy?" I started to gather to my feet.

"Ne pars pas. No rush. Enjoy!" He nudged my arm, pushing me back down into my chair.

"I can't," I answered. "My dad's expecting me home."

"Permit me to help ease your *difficultés*, oui?" He brushed past my rejection. "Allow me to offer you some wine until Wendy returns," he smiled too sweetly, extending the bottle to me.

"Where did she go?"

The Cajun ignored my question. "I hear you're new to our gang."

"Uh… I'm new to town," I corrected him.

"Ahheee!" he sang a catchy phrase known to the locals. "With that attitude, no wonder Wendy left," he belted a mocking laugh.

I snapped my head up. "Wendy's not coming back?" Icy tendrils trickled down my spine.

"No, problème. I got you covered. Laissez les bons temps rouler! Good times are here. Let's numb our troubles together, yes?" he winked.

I shoved the bottle from my face. "No! I don't drink." I shot him a pointed glare.

Though he didn't get my subtle hint. The Cajun leaned closer with breath smelling of rotten eggs. "Petite fille, we are delighted that you've come to join our coven."

"Whose coven?" my brows furrowed.

"Do you think you are here by chance?"

"Excuse me?" I asked.

"Let me show you, oui?" Without warning, the Cajun leaped to his feet. His skin paled like chalk, and blue veins jutted from his face and neck. "Do you think I am asking?" He drew back his lips, revealing two razor-sharp fangs.

Cold terror gripped me in its vile embrace. I bolted to my feet, knocking the chair to the sand. I threw my palms up, inching back. I forced myself to smile, etching away. "I-I-I have to go home."

The Cajun snared my arm and thrust the bottle into my face. "The wine is a mixture of mystical blood. Drink and experience immortality." Then cold evil shone in his black eyes. "Refuse and *die!*"

"Blood? And immortal life? What are you, a vampire?" I burst into laughter, verging on hysteria. "You're insane!"

Baring his fangs, the Cajun snatched me up into his arms and flung me to the ground. I landed on my head with a hard thud, jarring my brain into confusion.

When the haze lifted, horror pierced my mind. Throttling me, the Cajun squeezed his long fingers around my neck, choking the life from me. I opened my mouth to rake in air, but instead, he forced the crimson liquid down my throat.

It smelled of human waste and tasted like decay. I fought, gagging, spewing the foul liquid back into the Cajun's face. Each second passing, my mind faded into unconsciousness.

37

Suddenly the weight lifted, and air poured into my lungs. I rose up on my elbows, hacking up the remains. Sobbing and trembling, all I could think about was showering and burning the stained clothes that swaddled me in its stench. I spied the bottle beside me shattered into pieces, lying in a puddle of crimson. Relief welled up in my heart. Good! Diablo couldn't force anyone else to drink that foul stuff.

My eyes lifted, combing the parking lot. I noticed all but one bike was gone. The Cajun and the other biker had disappeared, leaving nothing but dust in their path. The only person in sight was the boy. My gaze locked onto his broad shoulders as he stood over my body like a guard dog.

He turned and spoke for the first time tonight. "Get up!" He bit out, and then in a rush, he grabbed my upper arm, hauling me to my feet. "I'm taking you home."

"Is this some sick prank?" I choked out, wiping my mouth with the back of my hand.

Ignoring my question, the boy dragged me by my arm across the paved lot. His hard eyes roamed the perimeter as if he expected the return of his friends.

We came to a halt at a Harley parked under the streetlight next to where Ella had parked her Beetle. Shivering uncontrollably, the sea breeze nipped at my skin with no mercy as I clung to my sheer shawl.

The boy paused, eyeing me from head to toe. In an attempt of chivalry, he shrugged off his leather jacket and tossed it over my shoulders. "Take my coat." His icy tone confused me. "You're going into shock."

"Thank you," I muttered through tears, avoiding eye contact.

He straddled his bike and then turned to me, extending his hand to mine. I accepted his kind gesture and climbed on back. "Hang on tight," he tossed over his shoulder. I nodded, locking my arms around his waist.

Fast and furious, topping a hundred miles per hour, I buried my face into his back, shutting my eyes tight and clinging to his firm waist for dear life. I distracted my mind by envisioning the warmth of my shower and my soft bed.

A short time later, we rolled up in front of my house. I hopped off the bike in a rush. A sense of excitement rippled through me. I made it home alive and safe. I'd plodded up the drive about midway when I remembered the boy. I turned back to him and forced a faint smile. "Uh... thanks."

His face grew solemn. "Stay away from Wendy and her gang."

"Do your friends play this sort of prank on people often? I mean feeding people fake blood." The sting of ire struck me.

He scratched his five o'clock shadow, looking at me from under his sooty lashes. "Stay away from them."

A sudden spark of sarcasm rolled off my tongue. "Maybe you should take your own advice."

I had marked those she-devils and their biker-buddies off the friend's list hours ago, but I was cu-

39

rious to hear his version. For all I knew, he could've been part of this insidious prank.

A sardonic expression tarnished his lush lips. "Nice meeting you, Micki O'Sullivan. And watch those corners at school." He gunned his Harley, speeding away into the night.

I stood wide-eyed, watching him fade away under the streetlamps that bathed the neighborhood with a gentle yellow glow. A chill glided under my shirt, and all at once, I longed for the safety of my house.

# Neighborhood Watch

I woke up to the door slamming. I had the strangest dream. Vampires of all things. The hype over fangs and drinking blood baffled me. I never understood the appeal. And after last night, the whole idea of drinking blood was so grotesque that I swore off watching horror films forever.

I shook off the effects of the dream, tossed the covers off my legs, and slid out of bed. The floor protested as my feet padded across the wooden planks and down the stairs. I made my way to the kitchen and stopped in the doorframe, staring at an empty room.

I'd forgotten. Dad had a business meeting this morning with the architect and his business partner. Dad had been spending a lot of time working. I supposed business was doing well.

Grandpa was off doing God knows what. He maintained a busy social life, but lately, he had been keeping time with the Dubrow widow. Grandpa said she'd cast a spell on him. I gagged at that notion. Not something I cared to dwell on.

I maundered to the kitchen window and gazed out onto our patchy green lawn. Everything was turning brown and orange. Fall had begun. A shaft of sunlight streamed through the window, giving the kitchen a warm, bright glow. A rare treat. Most of the time, the sky stayed gloomy, threatening rain. I inhaled a long sigh, realizing that I was now a permanent resident of Eastwick.

For a quick breakfast, I decided on a bowl of corn flakes. The breakfast of champions. After I made my cereal, I sat down at the table and scoffed a large spoonful in my mouth. I didn't understand what had gotten over me. I was suddenly ravenous. I couldn't eat fast enough. I shoved in another large bite when my eyes drifted to the newspaper laid across the table. My heart stopped on the first line. It read,

*Teenage Girl Gone Missing. Authorities Baffled.*

At once, my mind flooded with flashes of last night. If the boy hadn't intervened, I hated to think of the outcome. Chills pulled through me. Did Diablo and his buddies go too far on some other unsuspecting girl? I liked jokes as much as the next gal, but this prank crossed the line.

One thing for certain…Wendy and her sidekicks best steer clear of me. Fool me once, but the second time would be handcuffed in the backseat of a police car. Wicked Wendy deserved jail.

I stuffed the visions of last night to the back of my brain. Thankfully, the boy rescued me from a terrible fate. I got out unscathed, shaken, but unharmed. If I ever saw the boy again, I planned to express my full gratitude. Other than that, Wendy and her gang were on my crap list.

After breakfast, I threw on a pair of black jeans and a T-shirt. I found my favorite tennis shoes by the front door and tucked my skateboard under my arm, heading outside. Henry didn't like me traipsing off alone. Usually, old neighborhoods hosted gangsters. Though Henry might be right, I couldn't stay cooped up in the house all day. The day was too beautiful, in the low seventies, and an abundance of sunshine. An excellent opportunity to ride my board.

When I stepped outside, I drew in a long whiff of pine. I tilted my face toward the sun. Its generous warmth soothed my tired skin as I moaned above a faint whisper. "What a nice day."

I had skated past a couple of houses when my skateboard skidded over a pebble. I lost my footing and flew off the board, landing in a patch of grass. I fell on my butt as pain shot up my spine. I sat there a minute, shaking off the burn. When I dragged myself to my feet, I heard a snarky male voice dropping on my back. "Yo! Are you tryin' to tear up my lawn?"

I spun on my toes to face a light-skin, black teenager with very distinctive green eyes shooting darts at me. When my eyes met his gaze, I recognized him. It was the sourpuss on the bus.

"Excuse me?" I glared back at him. He acted as if I'd fallen on his precious lawn on purpose. "No need to get your panties in a bunch. No harm was done." The snooty boy had pushed my buttons.

"Huh, hmm." He tapped his angry foot, still glowering at me.

"Sorry. You want my blood too?" I poked back.

"Gul, I know you didn't say that to me in *my* neighborhood!" He rose a well-defined brow, pursing his lips.

"You sorta asked for it." I snatched my board, tossing him an ireful glance.

"If you weren't so stuck up, I'd invite you in for Kool-Aid."

I laughed. "I'm not a snob. I recently moved here," I defended myself. "And I don't like Kool-Aid."

"If you had bothered to speak to me in class, we could be hangin' out," he replied.

Then my eyes widened, realizing why he had been snarling at me on the bus. "You're in my calculus class!"

"You just now figurin' that out, boo?"

"Hey man, I'm sorry," I extended my hand to him. "I'm Micki O'Sullivan. Most call me, Mick." I smiled, hoping to ease his jilted feelings.

"I'm Elwood Candy. My friends call me Candy." He wiped his hand on the front of his shirt and accepted my offer. "I noticed you like hanging out with the witches."

"Witches?" I swallowed hard. "What do you mean?"

"Wendy and her girls are purdee wicked. They'll work their voodoo on you. People disappear hangin' with them."

The news article about the missing girl flashed in my mind. Cold chills knotted my gut. That girl could've been me. "Like, how?" What else did he know?

"Gul, I don't get within their reach to know everythang they do. When I see them girls in the cafeteria, I go to the opposite side. I'm terrified of those voodoo tramps and their black magic. They ain't gonna put me under a spell. I advise you to do the same."

"Don't worry," I scowled. "Wendy and her duo ruined any chance of friendship with me."

"What did they do?" The curiosity in his green eyes gleamed.

I craned my neck, checking to see if any suspicious person might be eavesdropping and then back at Candy. "Maybe, we should go inside."

"C'mon, let's get a soda. We can talk in my house. Mama's workin'." He grabbed my arm as his eyes roamed the neighborhood and led the way. The moment I stepped past the door, a faint scent of cinnamon struck my nose.

"Oh, your house smells good!" I took a whiff and savored it.

"That's my mama's cookin'," he bragged. "She makes the best sweet potato pie on this side of the bayou."

"What kinda pie?"

"Sweet potato," he repeated.

I tried picturing the pie, but all I came up with was a clump of orange potato in the center of raw dough. "I've never heard of a potato pie."

"We Louisianans love our pies. I was fixin' to slice me a piece. You want one too?"

"No, thanks. That's weird." I shook my head.

Candy wrinkled his nose. "Where y'at."

"Hmm, come again?" His accent was thick.

He stuck his lip out and said, "I. Said. Where. Is. You. From?"

"Oh!" I took in a sharp breath. "I'm from New York. Hell's Kitchen and Manhattan for a while."

"No wonder you talk funny." He twirled on his tennis shoes and disappeared in the kitchen. I heard him open the fridge, and moments later, he returned with a can of soda, cream. "Here, ya go." He handed me a cold drink.

It dawned on me how thirsty I was. I popped the top and guzzled down the whole can in nothing flat. Candy stared at me like I'd lost my mind. "Dang, gul! You wanna another?"

My ears blistered with embarrassment. "Thanks. I'm good." I wiped my mouth with the back of my sleeve and shrugged off the awkward moment. I didn't know what came over me. I felt like I had swallowed the Mojave Desert? My throat burned for thirst.

"Let's go to my bedroom upstairs." Candy motioned his hand for me to follow.

My eyes gave the living room a quick sweep. Though small with worn furniture, it was clean.

Much like my old house, Candy's home needed repairs. The house had to have been built in the early nineteen hundreds. Apart from its age, it had a woman's touch. Vases filled with crepe myrtle were placed all over the room, and a white, throw-blanket folded on the back of a couch. His house had a homey feeling.

Candy led the way. He held his bedroom door open for me as I entered and then darted to the window. His deep green eyes washed over the front lawn before closing the curtains.

Unlike the living room, his room resembled the aftermath of a tornado. Clothes cluttered the floor, and an empty bowl on his nightstand had crusty food around the rim and the stench of sour milk. I giggled internally. Messy bedrooms and boys went hand in hand.

"You seem a little paranoid," I asked as he flopped down on the edge of his bed.

"Dang straight, I am. Those witches are all over town, spying on people."

I sat down beside him. "I don't care for the trio, either." Sarcasm rode hard in my voice.

"You keep sayin' that." His trim brows dipped into a V. "Tell me what happened and don't leave nothin' out."

"You can't tell anyone. My dad can't find out, or else I'm grounded for life."

"Why would your dad ground you?"

I rolled my eyes. "I'm always on the brink of getting in trouble. It's my thing."

"A'ight." Candy crossed his chest with his index finger. "Not a word. Cross my heart."

I liked Candy. Judging, by his turquoise aura, he was a natural healer. I trusted that he'd go to his grave with my secret. So, I told him the whole terrifying tale of last night. He sat quietly, hanging onto every word until I finished leaving no stone unturned.

"Wow! Talk about Freaky Friday," Candy gasped.

"Yep, the scariest night of my life."

Candy cursed under his breath. "Where were the witches? Don't tell me they watched."

"Nope. Worse. The trio left me stranded."

Another stream of curses flew from Candy's mouth. "Them guls are evil mofos to prank you with fake blood! That's just downright nasty."

I grimaced, feeling naïve and stupid. "I should've known they were up to no good."

"How did you get home?" Candy's eyes brightened with curiosity.

"The biker that gallantly saved my life. He drives a candy-apple red Harley."

"What did that guy look like?"

"Uh, taller than me, sandy blond hair, piercing violet eyes, nice butt. Really cute." I bit my bottom lip.

Candy's eyes appled. "I know him! That's Valentine Breaux. He hangs out with the witches. That boy is a strange mofo."

"Yeah, he seems broody. But he wasn't like the other two bikers. He appeared more... *civil.*"

"Don't go gettin' a crush on him. He is part of those witches. He doesn't stray, either."

"I gathered that much." I shivered, thinking how stupid I was climbing in the car with those loser-girls.

"Valentine's tight with Wendy," Candy said. "Wendy's got some sorta spell on him. And those two girls, Ella and Cindy… it's like she cloned them. Weird as a mofo."

"Yeah, I noticed that too." I paused, thinking. "Do those two ever speak?"

"Hell, if I know. No one talks to me at school."

"What do you mean?" I asked.

"In case you haven't figured it out, I'm an oddball and gay," Candy said matter-of-factly.

"People don't like you because you're not straight?" I found that hard to believe. New Yorkers were open-minded. They were the melting pot of many diversities. I sorta thought folks had overcome prejudice. Guess not.

Candy's face dropped. "I stick out like a sore thumb. The south is slow when it comes to new age thinkin'. Most folks here in Eastwick don't know nothin' more than farming. Some folks don't even have a TV. Backward hicks, still living in the past. I'm probably the only boy wearing make-up in the parish."

"Well, I stick out too. Guess we can both be sore thumbs together. Besides, I could use a pointer or two on applying makeup." I paused. "They're stupid, yonno," I smiled, nudging Candy's shoulder.

"I have a feeling you and I are gonna be best buds." His caramel-colored face brightened.

"Best ever!" I laughed, tossing my hair over my shoulders. "Do you skateboard?"

"Uh… I say hell to the nah! I ain't breakin' none of my lovely bones or markin' up my delicate face, either."

I giggled, grabbing his sleeve. "C'mon! Walk with me, then."

* * *

**Later that evening**, Henry made it home right after Grandpa came staggering through the door. I decided to make dinner for my favorite two men. Henry had been kind enough to let me go out last night even though the beach party was a bust. I planned to keep last night's tragedy to myself. I feared Henry's reaction. I imagined he'd report them to the police and ground me forever. But all I cared about was putting this nightmare behind me. Although first, I intended to take a little detour and confront Wendy and her girls.

At home, the three of us gathered at the table. I made lemon chicken, green beans, creamed potatoes, and rolls with fresh sweet tea. Henry loved Barry's tea. Irish ran thick in his blood, though he had never been to Ireland.

Shortly after Grandpa moved here to the states, he met the love of his life, my grandmother, Martha Keys. When Grandma died of a stroke, Henry and Grandpa took it hard. We all did. Accepting her death took months for us to breathe again. I remembered her like it was yesterday. Full of life with her copper hair, she always carried a smile. My grandma touched everyone's heart.

Grandpa's eyes lit up. "My word, Lassie! I had no idea you cook." He stopped at my chair and leaned over, kissing me on the crown of my head.

"Thanks, Grandpa!" I smiled up at his wrinkled face.

"So, what did you do today?" Henry kicked off the conversation as he took a large bite of his potatoes.

I shifted in my seat, "Uh… I made a new friend. A neighbor, two doors down."

"That boy?" Henry asked.

"Don't be naive. If my granddaughter met a boy, he'd be knockin' the door down. She's beautiful like Martha," Grandpa added.

"Pop, I got this." Henry shot him a hushed glance.

"Alrighty. I was just sayin'," Grandpa mumbled into his plate.

"Uh… yeah. He's gay." I said for a bonus. I figured if I threw in the orientation, it might rest my dad's concerns about hanging out with him.

Grandpa's white brow shot up. "Aren't all young men your age happy? I was once a gay lad myself when I met your grandma."

I bit my bottom lip to keep from laughing.

Henry cut his eyes at Grandpa. "She meant that the boy… hmm, prefers a different type of companion." Henry held Grandpa's glint, hoping to convey the meaning.

Then as if a light went off in his head, Grandpa's mouth dropped open and shut as if his words lodged in his throat. "Oh," he merely muttered.

Henry appeared nonchalant as he took a bite of his chicken. "How did it go with your female friends last night? I heard you come home and on time."

"It went okay." I lifted my shoulder in a sharp shrug. I'd rather we talked about football instead, and I hated sports.

Henry paused, taking a drink of his tea, and then he asked, "Who's the biker?"

Pink suddenly blistered my face. "Uh… a friend of Wendy's. She had to leave in a rush, and her friend offered me a ride."

"You know you can call me. I don't mind."

Nerves fluttered my belly. "I know, but I'd forgotten my phone."

A line between Henry's brows deepened. "I don't pay your phone charges for you to leave it at home. I want you to have it in case of an emergency."

"I know." I secretly cringed to myself. "I totally forgot. Sorry, Dad. It was my first night out with friends." With any luck, Henry bought my lame excuse.

"Aye, modern technology is a grand thing for convenience," Grandpa spoke as he waved his butter knife in the air. "Trouble is that most young lads keep their heads so buried in those gobshite phones that they're missin' out on life."

"Pop, we totally agree. Eat your food before it gets cold."

"My food?" Grandpa's eyes glossed over with confusion as he twisted his neck, skimming the room. "Oh, there it is!" He stabbed his chicken with his fork. "I thought MacGyver had gobbled up me plate," he snorted, belting a deep laugh.

His sheltie, MacGyver, died six months ago. Grandpa was forgetful, much like he'd forgotten about Grandma Martha's death. From time to time, Grandpa spoke to Grandma Martha as if she stood over the stove, making a pot of tea. As time passed, Grandpa's mind declined, slipping away into another time. Henry and I stood by watching, unable to help. Grandpa had early stages of dementia. Every moment with him, I held dear to my heart.

Henry nudged me back to our conversation. "You like your new friends? What were those girls' names?" He bit into his baked chicken.

"Hmm, they're okay. I have more in common with the neighbor." Good answer, I internally patted myself on the back. "I'll probably hang out with Candy."

Henry's brow arched. "That's a girl's name."

I rolled my eyes, "Elwood is his first name. Candy is his last."

"Oh, that explains it," he laughed. "Hey, I thought tomorrow we might go downtown to the Square. There's a jazz band playing. You know, hang out with the old man and the older man." He whispered the last part about Grandpa.

I couldn't help but laugh. "That sounds like fun, Dad!"

# Without a Conscious

Early Monday morning, I met up with Candy at his house. I knocked on the door in a rush. I heard feet shuffling and hustling to the door. Candy swung the door open as he donned his windbreaker. "Why are you knockin' this early?"

My brows puckered. "With your attitude, no wonder you don't have friends." Irritation charged through me as I shoved past Candy into his house and spun on my feet, corn-colored hair twirling over my shoulders as I caught his gaze. "I gotta problem." I tugged down my collar, revealing purple thumb marks covering each side of my neck. "I don't know how I got past Dad and Grandpa."

"Dang! By the looks of those bruises, that biker was squeezing your neck like one malevolent mofo!" He leaned in, eyeballing the trail of dark bruises.

"What do I do?" Tears welled in my eyes. "I can't go to school looking like I'd been making out with the Hulk!"

"Yeah, you right! Them ugly marks look like giant hickeys." He lifted my hair, examining my neck. "C'mon! Let me work my magic, boo." He took my hand and led the way to his bedroom.

"I got the right stuff that will hide any blemish." He pulled out a drawer and snatched up a small round flat container. "This is my drag-queen makeup. Never leave home without it," he smiled, opening the container. "Now hold still." He smoothed the cool liquid over the bruises. The cream, cool to the touch, soothed my skin, though the makeup didn't stop the pain. Each touch stung as bad as a hornet's sting. "I didn't notice these bruises yesterday. They must've just popped up."

"My neck was sore, but that was all." I bit my bottom lip holding back a painful moan.

"Bruises always look worse before they heal." Candy stepped back, eyeing his artwork. "There! You can't even tell." His grin flashed wide, dazzling against his tawny skin.

"Really? You can't see the marks?" I snatched up a hand mirror off his dresser and held it up to examine my neck. "Do you have better lighting? I can't see."

"Nope. Don't worry. You look as good as new, boo." He hastily tucked the cosmetic container back in the drawer and grabbed my hand. "We gotta go! The bus is gonna be her' any minute." We made a mad dash downstairs and out the door in the nick of time. The bus rolled to a stop at the curb, brakes swishing, and doors swinging open for us to board.

When the bus picked up its last student and headed for school, my stomach started to knot. I was anxious to confront Wendy. I expected our conversation to get ugly fast. I hated the girl worse than the crater size potholes at Staten Island. Punching her in the nose didn't seem to be enough. I wanted to do severe damage.

"Hey, you must be daydreamin'?" Candy bumped me with his shoulder. "Don't worry about those girls. They have left you in the wind and movin' on to their next victim."

That idea didn't console me. "Those sociopaths need stopping before they injure anyone else."

"Boo, let that be someone else. Best be happy you didn't get your head chopped off. Leave 'em alone."

"I'm incensed that they think they can get away with this atrocity." Raw anger spilled over into my voice.

"Quiet. Do you want folks hearin'?" He swiped his eyes over the other students. Everyone appeared to be in a sleep-haze. Then adding the roar of the bus's engine and the thrumming of the large wheels churning underneath, I doubted anyone heard a word.

I shook my head and leaned in closer to Candy. "I have to report Wendy and her duo to the authorities."

"Don't be stupid! They'll come after you. Be happy that all you got were ugly bruises! At least those will heal in a day or two." His eyes fell to my neck, making me self-conscious.

"I thought you said your makeup covered the marks up?" I smoothed my hair over my neck.

"Your skin is lily-white," he pursed his lips.

I dug out a small mirror from my purse and opened it. I held it up to my neck and gasped. "Great! Just great!" I shoved the compact back inside. "I just now got demoted from rape girl to skank girl. I'm finished!"

Candy swatted the air and blew out a sharp breath. "No one is gonna think you're skank girl, but they might think you're a hickey girl," he snickered. "Wear your collar up. Ain't nobody gonna notice." He rolled his eyes. "Besides, most guys don't get past the boobs."

I scoffed. "What?"

"You're not exactly in my ballpark, but you got all the right stuff. Every boy at school is droolin' over you, gul."

"Thanks! But I don't want to be on every dude's radar. I hate attention. I'd rather fade into the wall."

"Not me. I wanna be a dancer. Talent runs in my family. My daddy was a part-time rapper." Candy's eyes drifted to the window.

"Where is your father now?" I asked.

"He disappeared. He went out to visit his Uncle Jim Bean, but he never made it there. The po-po found his car and a pack of Kools left in the seat. Keys still dangling in the ignition. He's been gone now for two years." His face dropped. The pain in his face was entrenched.

"I'm sorry." I stroked his shoulder.

He shrugged, looking at his feet. "Something happened to him. Daddy was a good man. He wouldn't have left us." He wiped a tear from his cheek.

"Hey, this weekend, let's do makeup and paint the town." I smiled, though in my heart I was hurting for my friend.

"Sure. That sounds like fun. I can take you to some cool places." He strained a smile.

We remained silent for the rest of the ride. I spotted some of the students giggling and cutting their eyes back at us. I didn't care. I was Candy's friend through thick and thin. I had his back, and he had mine.

We arrived at school ten minutes before the bell. Candy and I had calculus together, first class. I wished we had all our classes together. We headed for our lockers before we made our way upstairs.

When I had finished loading my books for the next round, I spotted the trio. Fury purled through me as I watched them approach. All three carted a devilish smirk as if they'd gotten away with murder. Loathing poured over me.

"Where did you go?" Wendy spoke up as her sidekicks remained quiet. "I went to the car to get my jacket, and when I returned, you were gone."

"You're kidding, right?" I glared at her as if she'd lost her pea-pickin' brain.

Cindy's squeaky voice peered from the three. "You could've at least told us you were leaving."

I choked out a shocked laugh, bouncing my dumbstruck gaze between them. "You intentionally left me!" I stepped into Wendy's face, our eyes even. "What sort of sick game are you playing?"

A flicker of wickedness glinted in her dark eyes. "I haven't a clue to what you're talking about." Wendy tossed her long, raven hair over her shoulders.

"If it hadn't been for your friend, Valentine, I'd be in the hospital or worse... *dead!*" I held my fists, white-knuckled, to my side as I bit back my boiling temper. "The three of you and that Cajun biker should be behind bars rotting for the rest of your pathetic lives." I shot blue shards at the two other girls and cut my eyes back at Wendy. "Aiding and abetting is a crime, but you probably know that already."

"Don't be ridiculous." Wendy grimaced. "Whatever those men did to you was on their own accord." Then she smiled darkly. "Besides, you have no proof!"

Whata liar! I bit out. "Stay away from me."

"Don't worry. We don't hang out with trash and weirdos," Wendy hissed as she took a step toward Candy.

I cut in front of her. "Leave him out of this!" I itched to knock her lights out. If she made one step closer, I swore I'd do it.

"What are you gonna do, beat us up?" All three girls cackled.

"That's an appealing idea, but I fear I might grow bored pounding your airhead against concrete. I'd rather report you to the police." Their laugh stalled at once, and scorn smothered their taunting. Three against one. They outnumbered me, but this New Yorker wasn't cowering.

"Watch yourself. You have no idea what you're dealing with." The peril in her black eyes confirmed the lengths she'd take. "See you 'round."

A stiff breeze tousled my hair as I stood back, eyeballing the triad turn the corner and disappear from sight.

Suddenly my lungs expanded, raking in oxygen as Candy rushed to my side. "You okay?" His face was etched with worry.

I nodded. "Yeah, I'll live."

"Boo, you stirred the lion's nest."

"Maybe. But I can't allow those girls to bully me." I caught Candy's gaze. "I won't let them pick on you, either."

"Pay them no mind."

"You're right about everything. Those three witches are dangerous."

"You best not forget that little tidbit. Those mofo witches ain't used to someone standing up to 'em."

The bell rang and our conversation halted as we hurried to calculus.

Lunch came and the halls filled with aimless chatter. Candy and I brought a sack lunch and headed for the cafeteria. Since Candy was short on cash, I bought him a Dr. Pepper and me a Coke. We found an empty table by the window and sat across from each other. "We should do our homework together tonight. You wanna come over for dinner?"

"Who's cookin'?" Candy pulled out his baloney sandwich and took a large chunk out of it.

I laughed. "Dude, that's rude!" I threw a potato chip at him.

"Gul, I can't afford to get poisoned."

"I know how to bake meatloaf."

"Do you put ketchup or tomato sauce on top?" One manicured brow arched challenging me.

"I don't know. I have to look up the recipe."

Candy burst into laughter, replying, "Boo, you better let me cook. At least I can boil water."

"Oh, shut up! I cook all the time."

Without warning, Candy's green eyes grew wide, staring over my head as a baritone voice bristled the back of my neck. "Oh, you can cook?"

Candy and I exchanged a startled glance, and then I twisted in my chair, gawking at the intruder. Heat flushed my cheeks when my eyes locked with *Valentine's* face. "I-I guess."

My best friend, the coward, held his mouth open like he was catching flies.

My eyes froze on his long, lean physique. His firm mouth slightly curled into a smile. A swath of blond wavy hair fell casually over his left eye, and a bold tattoo peeked from under his short sleeve on his right arm. I recalled the Celtic knot. He was stunning, almost too beautiful.

"May I join you two?" he asked.

I made a terrible attempt at a shrug. "I guess." My curiosity spiked. Although, judging by the people he ran circles with, I had my reservations. My spidey senses sat on the fence.

He pulled out the chair next to me and sat down, holding my gaze as if he and I were the only ones sitting at the table. His violet eyes roamed over me before he spoke. "The bruises on your neck look painful. Are you all right?" His stare dug deep.

"It hurts a little," I answered in a soft whisper.

He glanced at Candy and spoke in a hypnotic voice. "Can you give me a moment with your girl? I'll only be a minute."

Candy slid a quick glance at me and then back at Valentine. "Uh, okay." His nose wrinkled with ire. "But I'm standing right over there watching, pal." My dear friend puffed his chest out as he pulled himself from the table, taking a seat across the aisle. Valentine ignored the glower pointed at his back, keeping his eyes fixated on me.

"Huh... we haven't officially met." His lips curled into a faint smile. "I'm Valentine."

"Micki," I stated.

"Your boy worries about you. He can relax." There was a suspicious line at the corners of his mouth.

"Why should he trust you? You hang out with wicked Wendy and rapists," I accused. "You know that saying about the birds of a feather?"

"I've never had the pleasure of speaking to a bird." He flashed a pearly smile.

"And I don't need a little birdie whispering in my ear telling me that you keep bad company."

His thick brown brow arched. "Diablo had no intention of raping you."

"Of course not!" I jeered. "It was all a game. Pranking me with fake blood. Oh, I loved his phony fangs. And your girlfriend, Wendy, set all this up so you could have a laugh... *at my expense.*" I crossed my arms over my chest as betrayal pierced my heart.

"I'll admit my company is questionable, but you're clueless about the dangers that lurk in the shadows of Eastwick." His lips suddenly tightened. I must've hit a nerve.

"Did you know what Diablo was planning? Were you part of this disgusting prank?" Though Valentine stopped his friend from doing worse, I still considered him an accomplice.

"No. I had no idea. I usually don't get involved," Valentine diverted his eyes to the window. He became quiet, almost withdrawn as if he was struggling internally.

I pushed for more. "Then why did you stop your friend?" I shoved my sandwich and chips across the table, I'd lost my appetite.

Valentine's eyes churned with aggravation as he leaned into my ear and whispered, "I chose to intervene. Let's leave it at that."

"Are you as vile as Diablo?" Every fiber in my body urged me to run, but I had to know.

"At the moment, no. But I can't promise you what the future will hold." Valentine clamped his lips together. "Look! I'm here to warn you. Don't go to the police. It will only make the situation worse."

I gaped. "Wendy asked you to speak to me, didn't she?" My spidey senses screamed.

His lips hardened. "No." He inclined his head. "Yes! But it's not what you think. I care what happens to you."

I scoffed. "Liar! You don't want your friends in trouble." My eyes narrowed in dismay at his boldness. "You've got some nerve!"

"I am trying to keep things from escalating." Anger burned hell hot in his glint.

"I appreciate your help, but you needn't bother. I won't go to the police."

He captured my gaze and held it as if he were trying to gather my private thoughts. "How have you been feeling? Any strange dreams, thirsty more than usual?"

What an oddball thing to ask. "What?"

"Answer the question, please," he ordered.

"Why do you care?"

Valentine gave in to a dark smile that chilled my blood. "I may need to save your life again."

His cold words struck me like a bullet to the heart. "Don't trouble yourself. I'm fine. Go hang out with your gang. They seem to be more your type."

A smile ruffled his face, but it was more of a warning than humor. "We don't always get to choose our paths." He paused, entrapping my glare. "See you around, beautiful." He rose from his chair in one fluid motion, pushing his hands deep into his pockets. He nodded with a taunt jerk of his head, and without a word, he turned on his heel and strode to the door.

I watched in silence, unable to peel my eyes away as he walked with effortless grace, swift, full of virility, carrying himself with a commanding air of self-confidence.

"What did that mofo want?" Candy slid into his chair with agitation blistering his face.

Jarred from my thoughts, I turned my eyes to my friend. "Valentine came to warn me to keep quiet about Friday night." A wave of apprehension washed over me. "I got the feeling he was digging. He asked if I'd been thirsty. How weird is that?" I stared back at the metal doors that he had exited from.

"That's weird. Come to think about it, the first day we met, you chugged downed a soda like it was Fat Tuesday." Candy shrugged dismissively. "Then again, this is Louisiana. The state of weird and mofo weirder."

"You got that right," I said, mulling over Valentine's cryptic behavior. "He's a student here, right?"

"Kinda. Valentine sorta comes and goes as he wishes."

"How does he get away with missing school?"

"He's among the privilege. Yonno, rich kids."

"Valentine's rich?" I didn't get that vibe from him.

"Duh, he drives a classic Harley." Candy bugged his eyes at me.

I dumped my sandwich and chips back into the brown sack and rolled it up. The sight of meat and red tomatoes made me feel like barfing, but strangely my stomach continued to rumble.

"Gul, you okay?" Candy's wary eyes washed over me.

"I'm fine." I leaned back, suppressing a sigh. "I just had the strangest conversation." I suddenly wrapped my arms around my waist, fighting off an icy shiver.

"Dang!" he squinted his eyes. "You're lookin' more pasty than normal. Your blue lips are worryin' me, boo. Let me take you to the nurse's office."

"No. I'm fine. Only two more hours to go before school is out." I laid my head in the palm of my hands and shut my eyes tight against a sudden gut-wrenching spasm. Like waves slamming against the harbor, pain consumed me.

"No, gul. I'm taking you to the nurse. I can get my cousin to take you home."

"Candy, I don't want to be alone. Grandpa's off fishing and my dad's at work. I'd rather stay here." I clutched at my stomach and doubled over.

"You ain't goin' home alone." He leaped from his chair. "I'm gonna go with you." He wrapped his arm around my waist, throwing my arm over his shoulder, lifting me to my feet. At once, I felt weak at my knees.

"Boo, you're burning up. C'mon, lean on me." He gripped my waist, holding me up as we stumbled our way down the hall.

Somewhere between the cafeteria and the nurse's office, I must've fainted. When my eyes fluttered open, I was stretched out on a cot, and Valentine was standing over me. His eyes were deep with worry.

My brows furrowed as confusion clawed through my mind. "Where am I?" I mumbled.

"You were unconscious." His fingers brushed a strand of hair from my face.

I heard Candy speak, sounding angry. "Hey, fella! I got her!"

Valentine cut his eyes at my friend. "It'd be better if I took over from here. Trust me, you don't want to be near her when she crosses."

"What is that supposed to mean?" My friend's voice struck back.

"Quiet!" Valentine hissed. "You'll bring attention to yourself."

"Stop!" I spoke hardly above a whisper. "Don't hurt him." I tried to sit up but dropped back down, swooned with dizziness.

Valentine turned back to me. "You want your friend safe, then he needs to step aside. Let me take care of you."

Abruptly, my spidey senses blasted like sirens. I believed Valentine. Pinning my glint to Candy's face, I touched his arm and whispered, "It's okay. I'll call you later. I promise." My heart tugged. He had the look of unmitigated fright, but he nodded and stepped back. A curt smile crossed his mouth, and I smiled back, reassuring him that I'd be fine.

"I need to get you out of here before the nurse returns." Then Valentine scooped me up into his strong arms and stepped out of the tight room. He peeked down both sides of the hall, and then swiftly moved out into the foyer heading toward the main entranceway.

Soon I heard the doors slamming behind us, and the sharp sensation of the cold wind coasting up my shirt and whipping through my hair as rapid footfalls flooded my brain. I had to have been delirious. Nothing made sense.

Minutes later, I was lying flat on my bed. Pain, godawful pain, licked through my body. "My skin is burning," I mumbled.

Unable to grasp what happened next, my clothes were peeled off down to my bra and panties. Then Valentine lifted me into his arms again and immersed my body in a tub of ice water. I gasped, shivering, fighting back, hands flailing to no avail. The freezing water was more than I could bear, and yet it soothed my singeing skin.

"Relax." Valentine's musical voice penetrated my muffled brain. "The ice will cool down your fever. Be still." He consoled me as he sat on the edge of the tub, dabbing a cool cloth over my forehead.

"W-w-what's wrong with me? M-m-my skin hurts."

He stroked my hair. "You're changing," he spoke barely above a whisper.

"C-changing..." All at once, my thoughts and surroundings faded to blackness.

# Riddled

**I woke** with a start, bolting to a sitting position in the dim light. A soft gasp of surprise escaped my lips as a stiff chill hovered in the air, making me shiver. My eyes swept across my bedroom. Complete quiet. Not a peep throughout the house. No sign of Candy or Valentine.

Embarrassment heated my cheeks as I quickly threw back the covers. Finding my clothing still intact, I huffed out a breath of relief. I was dressed in a white T-shirt and my favorite pajama pants.

I dropped back down on my pillow, staring at the skylight. My fever had devoured my strength, leaving me weak. The agony setting my skin on fire had ceased, and now cool to the touch, I appeared back to normal. Or did I dream this?

Candy came to mind, and I grabbed my phone off the nightstand and hit his number. On the first ring, he answered. "Gul, are you okay? I've been worried sick." The disquiet in his voice was on the verge of tears.

"I'm better. Can you come over? I don't feel like being alone."

"Say, no, mo'!" Shortly after my phone clicked, I heard footsteps climbing the stairs. A familiar voice bellowed. "You dressed?" All this time, he'd been out-side perched on my doorstep. I wondered how long he'd been waiting.

"I'm decent," I yelled back as his tennis shoes tromped louder.

In the next breath, he pushed through my bedroom door and bounced down on the edge of the bed. "Boo, I've been nothin' but sick with worry. That mofo booted me out. Are you all right?"

I reached over and hugged my friend. "I'm okay now. A little tired." My voice was a little shakier than I would've liked. "Did you see Valentine? What did he say?"

"Other than threatening to kick my ass, he didn't say a mofo thang." Concern shone in his eyes like twin candles in the night.

"How long did he stay?" I asked.

"At least two hours. I perched on your steps. I told that mofo I wasn't leaving!"

"I remember Valentine saying something about crossing. Do you recall anything about that?"

"Uh… no, but he acted like my life was in danger hangin' 'round you."

"That's weird. What do you think he meant?" I stared back at Candy.

"Heck if I know. But it sure does feel eerie." Candy rubbed the goosebumps across his arms.

"Do you know where Valentine lives?"

Candy's eyes bulged with shock. "You gotta be outta your ever-lovin' mind? Stay away from that mofo."

"Believe me! I wish I'd never met him, but I think he knows what's happening to me." I bit my bottom lip. "Will you please help me?"

Candy froze. His face was painted in fright. Silence rested between us for a brief minute, and then he answered, "I'll help you, but first let's find him at school. He's less likely to chop our heads off on campus."

I reached over and threw my arms around my dear friend. "You're the best friend a girl could ever have!"

Candy jumped back. "I know I'm lovely, but don't go gettin' your slobber on me. I hate wrinkled shirts. And, whatever you got is one germ I ain't catchin'." He held his palm up in defense.

I cackled out loud, laughing.

Later, Candy left for home. He had to tidy up the house before his mom got off work. After I watched him enter his home safely, I locked my door. Ever since that night at the beach, a sinister feeling clung to me like frozen ice to a bridge. I shook my head, denying my unnecessary paranoia.

* * *

Grandpa made it home right at dusk empty-handed. "No bloody fish bitin' today," he grumbled in Irish, dragging his heavy feet down to the basement.

Henry came home late from work. Looking at his drawn face, I assumed his day didn't turn out any better than mine. For dinner, I ordered pizza. Pepperoni, my favorite. I threw a couple of slices in the microwave and brought it to Henry with a cold Budweiser. He plopped down on the couch; his arm rested over his eyes. "Dad, you want some aspirin for your headache?" I set the plate down on the coffee table, along with his beer.

Without moving, Henry mumbled, "That would be nice. Killer headache."

"I'll be right back." I rushed down the hall to the guest bathroom. I found a full bottle in the medicine cabinet. I snatched it up and went back to the family room. I placed two white pills on his plate. Then I eyed the beer. He might not want alcohol with medicine. Unsure if beer would affect the aspirin but just in case, I poured Henry a cold glass of water. "Dad, I thought you might want water instead."

"Thanks, jellybean. Water is fine." He peeked out from under his arm. "How was your day?"

Oh, Jesus! Should I tell him? Better cover my tracks. "I got sick today and came home early."

Henry dropped his arm to his side and sat up, eyeballing me from head to toe, brows furrowed. "Are you sick?"

I shook my head, no. "I'm better now. I ran a fever earlier. Thought you should know. I didn't want you thinking I'd skipped school."

His body jiggled, laughing. "That's the first." He eyed the aspirins and then tossed his head back and popped two pills in his mouth, washing them down with his water. "Thanks for bringing me a plate." He picked up a slice and bit off about half of it. He chewed his food for a minute, then he asked. "Are you liking Eastwick High? Fitting in?"

"It's still new. Candy's turning out to be a good buddy." I sat down next to him on the couch and folded my legs under me.

"He's a good kid, but what about girls? You know, girl stuff," he winked, taking another bite.

"Dad, girl-stuff isn't all that great. I'm happy hanging out with Candy."

"I'm glad you're buddies. He seems like a good kid. I think his mom works two jobs. Have you met his mother?"

I wrinkled my nose. "Nope, not yet."

"I think you should make an effort. Since we had Candy over for dinner last Wednesday."

"I will, but his mom is never home."

All at once, Henry's eyes dropped to the coffee table. His brows drew into a worried-line. I wiggled in my seat, watching. I knew exactly what had snared his attention. Henry gathered the newspaper in his hands and began to read the article to himself. After a brief moment, he drew in a sharp breath as his glint shot up at me. "A kid is missing. Police think it might be an abduction." Alarm glittered in his eyes. "From now on, I want you home before dark."

"Dad, the only person I hang out with is Candy. I'm safe."

"All right. Just promise me that when you two are out that you stick close together. There's safety in numbers. And… if you go anywhere, I want to know the details. Keep your phone on you at all times and make sure it's charged."

"Okay, no problemo," I smiled to ease his concerns. If he knew about my close encounter, he'd come unhinged. Maybe the right thing would be to tell him, but I couldn't be homebound right now. I think it was best to keep my secret to myself for the time being.

"Has your mom called?" He took a drink of his water and swiped the remote from the coffee table.

"Hey! I was going to watch a movie."

"I think the keyword is … *was*." A flash of humor flickered in Henry's eyes. "Well?"

"Nope, Mom hasn't bothered." I didn't feel like talking about Joan or my stepfather. Every time Phil yelled at me for whatever reason, Mom defended him. It had gotten to a point where we did more shouting than talking. "Yonno, Phil shoved me into a wall during one of our shouting matches." I might be a crappy stepdaughter, but Phil had no right to put his hands on me.

"That's why you're here, jellybean." Henry finished off his last bite and started on the second slice.

"Dad, I don't want to go back. I can't stand Phil."

"You're not the first kid to dislike a stepparent." He playfully reached over and ruffled my hair up.

"Dad, stop," I giggled, fixing my hair in place.

"I don't want you to go back either. You're here with me 'til you go to college and even then, you'll have a home here. Always, kiddo."

My eyes misted. "Thanks, Dad," I swallowed the lump in my throat and changed the subject. "Can I go see Candy?"

"Don't you have homework?"

"I don't know. I left early, remember?"

"What you mean to say is that you want to go hang out with your BFF."

"Uh... I'd like to do that too." At least I told the partial truth. I did need to get my homework. Of course, Candy probably didn't know either.

"Why don't you call your friend and have him email you the lessons?" Henry hesitated. "I don't want to alarm you, but the kid missing, a young girl a couple of years younger than you, lives only two streets behind us."

"Oh, wow!" Fear welled up in my throat.

"Kids go missing even in small towns." Disquiet crossed Henry's face. "Do you know a kid by the name, Susan Wallace?"

"The name doesn't ring a bell." The thought of any girl going missing gnawed at me like a rat in my guts.

"Her dad, James, works for me. I can't imagine how torn the family must be," Henry grimaced. "Listen, it doesn't make me feel good leaving you here alone all the time. Even when Pop is here, he's not." Henry blew out an exasperated sigh. "I don't know what I'd do if something happened to you."

"Dad, nothing's going to happen to me." I smiled as I leaned in and kissed him on the cheek. "I'll give Candy a call." I played it cool, but underneath, panic was rioting within me.

Upstairs in my bedroom, I hit Candy's number. On the first ring, he answered. "Boo, I'm sleepin'."

"I'm sorry. I thought you might know if we have any homework?"

"How am I supposed to know? I left school when you did." I pictured him pursing his lips.

"Hey, be careful whenever you leave your house. Dad told me a young girl is missing two streets behind us." I lay back on my bed, staring out the skylight. The stars glistened as if everything was well in the world. "I'm scared. I have this sick feeling that Valentine and Wendy are involved. I can't let this rest. I plan to find Valentine and get to the bottom of this nightmare."

"Who is the missing gul?" Candy asked.

"Hmm... Susan Wallace. I think."

"Man! I know her. Sorta. She's in middle school, about thirteen."

"Holy crap! This has me shaken." My stomach knotted.

"It's got me rattled too."

"There's something weird about Valentine. He's not... *normal*."

Candy quieted for a second. "Tomorrow, we'll go find that mofo and ask him whatz up."

"You're willing to help me?" I was surprised by his willingness.

"Yep! We family now."

I smiled into the phone. "Yeah, family."

"Hey, my mama made groceries today. She's cookin' some of her famous gumbo. Why don't y'all come over for dinner tomorrow night?"

"I'd love to, but Henry works late. Can I have a rain check?"

"No problem. I'll save you a piece of sweet potato pie."

"Sounds good." Just thinking of food pained my stomach.

"Yo… I gotta go. Mama's yellin'. See you at the bus stop in the mornin'."

I heard a click, and the screen went black. I tapped it to see the time. Bold numbers flashed 11:00 p.m. Bedtime. With a sharp huff, I dragged myself into my small bathroom and turned on the shower. It only took a minute for the water to reach the perfect temperature. I tossed my clothes in the hamper and climbed inside, standing under the water. I inhaled the day away, letting the small steamy beads pound my tired body. I soaped up using Caress, lavender-scented, my favorite.

When the water ran cold, I stepped out and wrapped my towel around my body. I went to my dresser and dug out the first pair of pajamas I found.

A gentle breeze drifted through the windows as I climbed in bed under the covers and picked my book off the nightstand. I wrinkled my nose at its title, *Carrie*. I placed it back. Stephen King was my favorite author, but maybe I should hold off reading horror books for now. I threw the covers off, tucked my pillow under my arm and snatched my blanket, heading out my window onto the roof. This was my favorite spot in the whole wide world. Hidden back from anyone's notice, gazing at the vast stars. My own little piece of heaven.

Wrapped in my blanket, I stretched my hands behind my head. I drew in a deep breath, enjoying the delicate scent of pine and crepe myrtle. Crickets were humming in the trees, and most of the lights in the neighborhood were out. Only a streetlight shed its soft glow over our lawn. I craned my neck, looking at Candy's bedroom window and noticed a light burning. I started to text him, but then, I remembered he'd gotten in trouble for being on the phone. I exhaled a long sigh and settled back down on my pillow, gazing at the stars.

It suddenly hit me. I was happy here. Dad worked long hours, but he stayed plugged in. He didn't mind taking time with me. And Grandpa, though his mind might be slipping, I treasured my time with him. Then there was Candy. I'd never had a closer, loyal friend than him. I hoped our friendship lasted forever. When I lived with Joan and Phil, I struggled to fit in with kids my age. I was sort of a misfit. I didn't mind being the odd person out. I guess that was why Candy and I were such a good fit. I was okay with that. And despite what others might think, I wasn't compromising myself to please someone else.

Then my mind drifted to Valentine. I think he was kinda like me, a loner. Apart from his alluring features, I found him a complete mystery. He couldn't be much older than me, eighteen maybe. Though, I sensed an air of command that exuded from him. He wasn't the run of the mill sorta guy. A boy among criminals, yet he seemed to care what happened to me. He saved my life twice now. Was he my savior? "Nah!" I giggled. I'd been reading too many fantasy books. Although he captured my curiosity. I'd never seen anyone with his eyes. Violet. Not blue or green but a soft purple. His skin was perfect too, a deep tawny glow. Almost too perfect.

I twirled a strand of hair around my forefinger unconsciously, wondering. I sensed a hidden danger within him. Yet, he didn't frighten me, like I could trust him. Apart from other boys, I sensed a distinctness about him. A ruggedness, perhaps? I always liked mystery and intrigue. Taking a risk was exciting. But I got the feeling Valentine's edge was stepping across the line. Goosebumps popped up over my skin, making me shiver. I was playing with fire, but despite my crush, I had to find out what was in that bottle and what he meant about me crossing.

That night I twisted in my sleep. Dreams of sharp teeth coming at me in a dense forest. Faceless laughter and footfalls chasing me. I ran mindlessly, foliage slapping my face, tripping over vines. My legs burned with pain as fear tore through my body. I was lost, unable to find safety. Long-cold-fingers kept pulling at me, yanking my hair, touching my skin. I kept running as fast as my legs could carry me, denying my lungs oxygen.

# Trap

Candy and I arrived at school early the next morning. I noticed the quiet throughout the bus today instead of the usual chatter. The odd stillness unsettled my nerves as I thought about the missing girl that lived in our neighborhood. All the more reason I had to find Valentine.

After we stopped at our lockers, loading up for the day, we took off in the direction of the park next door.

"I'm not sure meeting Valentine at Eastwick Park is a great idea. It's too secluded." When I was a small child, playgrounds with swings and merry-go-rounds terrified me. Even now, at the magical age of seventeen, my phobia forged on.

"That's where he hangs out with his buddies." Candy halted in the middle of the hall and faced me. "Look! We don't have to do this. Let's eat breakfast and forget him." He shifted his feet with his hands shoved in his jean-pockets.

"Yeah, you're right." I bit my bottom lip. "Hey, why don't you go on, and I'll meet you in a minute. I forgot something in my locker."

"What did you forget?" He eyed me suspiciously.

"Do you really want to know?" I learned if you mention girls' stuff, it freaked boys out. Even a gay dude.

He threw his palms up. "Say no mo! I'll meet you in the cafeteria." He reeled in his untied tennis shoes and trotted down the hall. I watched as a wary expression settled on my face. He would've come regardless of his reservations. Despite my pleading earlier, this was my problem. No point in putting both of us in harm's way. I headed in the opposite direction and out the front entrance.

As I neared the edge of the park, my heart kicked up, pounding against my ribs. My eyes peered through the stand of dense trees, catching several people sitting at a picnic table. I spotted a candy-apple red Harley in the parking area. I recognized it right away. It belonged to Valentine. A rush of excitement flurried through me, along with dread.

Though my excitement crashed when I locked eyes on Wendy's face. Perched on top of a picnic table, her skirt hiked up to her thighs, she sat with her legs crossed. Her black hair spread over one shoulder. The mousy hair girl, Cindy, was seated beside Wendy. But the freckled face girl, Ella, was absent and so was Valentine. My hope plunged to the ground.

Regardless of how creepy Wendy made me feel, I refused to give her the satisfaction of running me off.

81

I thrust my shoulders back, held my chin high, and marched right up to her. "Where's Valentine?" I demanded. No time for joking.

"Why do you ask?" Wendy glowered at me, not bothering to hide her disdain.

I was accustomed to someone disliking me. It was her inadequacy of empathy that bothered me. Flashbacks of the beach pummeled my mind. I inhaled a deep breath of courage and looked her straight in the eye. "Not that I'm obligated to explain myself, but I need to talk to Valentine," I smiled darkly.

"I heard you were sick yesterday. What a shame. Several are out sick or … *missing*." The tone of her sinister voice sent chills down to the bone. A strong sense came over me that Wendy and her insidious posse had something to do with those missing kids.

I instantly wanted to body slam her. "A girl near my home has vanished. Why do I get the feeling you're involved?"

She burst into laughter. "You think if I were guilty that I'd tell you?" Wendy glanced at Cindy as they both chimed in laughter.

Eerie was stamped all over those girls' faces. They were guilty. But I couldn't prove it. Right now, I had my own demons. "Where is Valentine?"

"He'll return when he's done." Wendy nodded a sharp chin toward the restrooms. "Or be my guest if you wanna disturb his morning delight?" She flashed a seedy grin.

I leered at her, crossing my arms over my chest. I understood exactly what she meant. "I can wait." I tried to hide the sudden tug at my heart. Valentine with another girl bothered me more than I cared to admit. But I'd go to my grave before I'd share my feelings with Wendy. I stalked over to a tree and leaned against it. I wasn't about to join those two at the table.

Wendy leaned into Cindy's ear, whispering. The two girls glanced up at me, giggling. Apparently, they were taunting me. I rolled my eyes, glaring back at them. A sting of regret kicked up my pulse. I held my breath, hoping I hadn't made a rash decision. I stood there eyeing the girls suspiciously, wishing I owned a can of pepper spray.

As I picked at my nail polish, I heard a faint jingle. I glanced up and caught Valentine swaggering back buckling his belt. Ella was right behind him. Jesus! Hooking up in a park's restroom was gross. I caught Wendy's smirk, and I wanted to throttle her. Instead, I planted my feet.

When Valentine made his way to Wendy's side, she tossed over her shoulder at me. "You have a visitor." She cut her eyes at me as the three vixens joined together snickering.

Valentine snapped his head up, and our eyes collided. The look of surprise glistened in his glint for a brief second, and then the familiar mask descended once again.

He stalked over to me, his expression was taut and derisive. "What are you doing here?"

"I need to talk to you," I spoke up firmly. I refused to chicken out now.

Valentine kept his back to the trio, his voice low. "I told you not to come around these girls. Do you ever listen?"

"I listen to my daddy," I smiled sweetly.

He glowered as if dealing with a temperamental child. "I'm not playing."

"Neither am I," I said. "Look! I want to know what you meant about crossing. I can't stop thinking about that night. I'm having nightmares." I paused to compose myself. "What was really in that red-ruby bottle? Was it wine? Diablo held on to it like it was some sort of precious artifact."

As soon as the last word slipped my mouth, Wendy and the other two girls snapped their heads up.

Valentine glanced over his shoulder and slid his eyes back to me. "Let's get out of here!" Without a word, his fingers bit deeply into my arm as he pulled me in the direction of his bike.

"I'm not leaving!" I dug my heels into the soil and jerked my arm free. "I can't miss another..."

Valentine interrupted, "Come with me if you want to hear the truth."

"Fine! But this is *kidnapping*," I hissed in his face, jabbing my finger into his chest.

A muscle flicked angrily at his jaw, but he didn't reply, which irritated me immensely. At that moment, I hated him.

After he threw his leg over his Harley, I climbed on the back and awkwardly snaked my arms around his waist.

He started the engine as it sputtered to life. Soon, off we sped onto the slick highway. I closed my eyes, terrified. He was reckless with no care to the outcome if we crashed.

We drove down a narrow dirt road. The Cypress trees dotted the way as they spread their generous shade. In the background, I heard the river roar with life, almost drowning out the bike's hum. The sky had grown darker since we'd left the park. The smell of rain lingered in the air. And the realization of being stuck in the middle of nowhere with a boy I hardly knew troubled me worse than getting mugged in Central Park. Did I not learn my lesson the last time? I huffed angrily at myself.

We came to a halt off the dirt road onto a green patch of low weeds. I spotted the river past the tree line. A faint smell of fish wafted from the bank.

Valentine killed the bike, and we dismounted. Not wasting any time, I was abruptly caught by the elbow and firmly escorted toward the river. I squirmed from his grip, screaming, "No! You're not going to drown me."

He halted, cutting his eyes at me. "I'm not planning to hurt you," his nostrils flared. "I've been trying to protect you, but you make it hard."

"I don't want your help!" I bit back. "I saw you with Ella," I blurted out into his pigheaded face, jealousy swallowing my fear.

He averted his eyes at the river, raking his fingers through his golden curls. I stood with my hands on my hips, waiting to hear his answer.

Valentine faced me; his angry voice stabbed the air. "I'm doing everything in my power to make this transition go smoothly for you."

"Are you hooking up with Ella?" I blurted out. I had to know.

"What?" His face twisted with hesitancy. "Why do you think I'm sleeping with her?"

"You were buckling your belt."

"At the park?" His eyebrow raised inquiringly.

"Yes!" I spat.

"I was taking a piss. Ella was in the women's restroom."

"According to Wendy, you were getting your morning delight."

"It sounds like you're jealous." His eyes grew openly amused.

"Don't be stupid. Are you sleeping with the enemy?"

Valentine reached out, drawing me into his arms, his breath flushed my cheeks. "I want you to listen to me." His eyes glowed with a savage inner fire. "The substance in the bottle wasn't wine. It was blood."

I laughed at the absurdity. "Why would your friend force-feed me blood? It doesn't make sense!" I cringed from the visions of that night.

"You need to listen!" Valentine cursed under his breath. "Your body is changing. The more you understand, the easier you can cope with the crossing."

"Crossing?" I inched back, but Valentine kept up with my step, glaring at me, holding my gaze captive.

"Yes," he bit out. "Have you ever heard of the un-dead?"

An electrifying shudder reverberated through me. "Are you trying to sell me some stupid vampire tale?" I think I rode off with a maniac.

"Where do you think those stories come from? They're not some writer's imagination. Vampires are real, sweetheart."

"Stop teasing me. There is no such thing."

"Have you forgotten Diablo?"

"How could I? He's in my nightmares." Chills skirted up my arms.

"You know so little," he snarled. "Do you even know what Wendy and the girls are?"

I snorted a laugh. "Yeah, witches with broomsticks up their butts."

Valentine scoffed. "Good one but not quite. They are watchers. They find prospects for our coven."

"Prospects like me?" Alarm struck my chest.

"Yes, like you," he whispered.

It just got real. My breath lodged in my throat. "Do you k-kill people?"

He turned his back to me. Uncomfortable silence wedged between us.

"Did you and your gang kill that missing girl?" I whispered. "Her name is Susan Wallace."

"Let's go!" Valentine snapped as he stalked past me to his bike. I quickly followed.

When he reached his bike with me right behind him, he spun on his heels, lips turned down into a hard frown. "The night Wendy brought you to the beach, I knew what Diablo was going to do. I'm sorry." His lips flattened. "I lied to you, but I wasn't part of their scheme."

I stepped back, gaping. "You knew?" Betrayal whipped through me like a sharp blade.

"Yes," he growled. "Listen, I may hang out with them, but I've never hurt anyone. Not yet." Those last two words iced my blood.

"Not yet? What does that mean?"

"It means we have more in common than you think. We're both changing. Only for me, my time is running out."

"I don't understand. You're not making sense." I shoved past my fright and asked, "Did Diablo or any of your friends kidnap that missing girl?"

Valentine looked off toward the river, and then in a fury, he punched the wind. "We gotta go." With light speed, he mounted his bike and ordered sharply, "Get on." I knew the conversation was over. Without further ado, I climbed on the back.

On the ride back, he followed the speed limit, but the tension between us was by far worse than his daredevil driving. Valentine's words haunted me. What did he mean, "*Not yet*?" Did Wendy and Diablo have something to hold over his head? He may be wild and unchained, but he had a compassionate nature, unlike his comrades. I wished I could read Valentine's aura, but I saw nothing. And my efforts to get Valentine to explain failed miserably. I wanted the truth, not some stupid fairytale.

By the time we'd arrived back at school, my hair and clothes stuck to me, saturated from the drizzle—a steady icy drip, not enough to call it rain but enough to make you miserable. Valentine rolled up to the entrance and stopped to let me off. I happily slid off and headed in the building, but his sobering voice stopped me in my tracks.

"You're changing, Micki O'Sullivan. Before long, you're going to be exactly like Diablo and Romeo." He called out merely above a whisper.

I twirled in my boots and glared at him like he'd lost his mind. "What does that mean?"

"You might want to steer clear of humans when it happens."

"Dude, you have gone freakin' crazy!"

A sardonic smirk caressed his lips. "Nah, I'm waiting for you to join me, sweetheart." His violet eyes held my breath. As though lured into a trance, I stood trapped, spellbound, unable to move.

When he dropped his hold, I jumped back, nearly losing my balance. In dazed exasperation, I managed to enter the building. Racked with shivers, school was out of the question for me today. I ached for the safety of my bed.

I made my way down the hall. When I reached the nurse's station, I found Nurse Jones on the phone. I hung back in the hallway until she finished with her private conversation. By the sound in her voice, it was apparent that I'd walked in on an argument. I knew that tone far too well from my parents. As soon as Nurse Jones ended the call, she called my name.

Though her voice appeared more relaxed, the deep lines across her forehead revealed otherwise. "What can I do for you, Micki?"

"I'm sick to my stomach. I feel feverish too." I held my tummy and twisted my face to make it more believable.

"Oh, dear." The nurse eyed me from head to toe. "Well, no wonder. You're dripping wet. Here, have a seat and let me have a look at ya," she smiled. I took a seat in the chair next to her desk as she placed a thermometer in my mouth. Beads of sweat collected over the bridge of my nose while at the same time, I shivered.

After a few seconds, the meter beeped, and the nurse took it from my mouth. "Well, you don't have a fever. Actually, it's low. 96.5. Some folks run low, nothing to worry about. But I'm sending you home. Do you have a ride?" She patted my shoulder.

"My dad, but my phone got wet. May I use the school's phone?"

"Sure, be my guest." Nurse Jones pointed to the desk phone.

"Thanks." I smiled and grabbed the phone, punching the keys to Henry's cell. Glad I'd memorized his number.

After two rings, I heard his voice. "Hello."

"Dad, sorry to bother you at work, but can you give me a ride home? I'm not feeling well."

Henry paused for a second. "No problem. I'll be there shortly."

"Thanks, Dad." Then the phone went dead.

"Sweetie, do you need to lie down?" the nurse asked in a soothing voice.

"I'm fine. I'll wait here," I smiled.

"Let me help warm you up." The nurse turned on her heels and headed off down a narrow hall. I heard a door creep open and then close. In less than a breath, she returned with a small blanket in her hands. "You look a little chilly. This will help." She spread out a small white blanket and threw it over me.

"Thank you." I pulled the cover over my shoulders. It felt like the cold had penetrated all the way down to my bones. The blanket helped to soothe my shivering.

By the time Henry drove up with a concerned father's face, the rain had begun pouring buckets. I attempted to rest his worries. "Dad, I'm fine. I'll crawl under the covers and sleep it off. It's nothing," I said as I hurried to open the truck's door on my side.

Henry stood over me, holding his coat above my head, calling out over the drumming rain. "This is twice in the same week, Mick. I should take you to the doctor." Worry oozed in his voice as he shut my door and rushed to his side.

"Can we postpone the doctor's visit?" I asked as Henry leaped in the truck and slammed the door. "If I'm not better by tomorrow, I'll go then. Please," I begged. I didn't feel like getting prodded by some fat-nosed doctor. Just give me my bed and *Netflix*.

Henry threw his saturated coat behind the seat and then rested his eyes on me. The expression on his face was a clear sign he was struggling with the proper protocol. Confusion rode hard on his shoulders as he tried to decide. "How high is your temperature?"

"I'm actually below the norm. After a little sleep, my upset stomach will be gone." I smiled but not too much. I really didn't have the energy for school today.

Henry ran his palm over his face and scratched his day-old whiskers. He did that whenever he was indecisive. This would be when Joan stepped in. Since she wasn't here, Henry was on his own. "Do you know how to read a thermometer?" he asked. His lips were tight and face nettled with fret.

"Yep, Mom taught me."

He grappled a loud sigh. "Against my better judgment, I'll wait until tomorrow. If you're still not feeling well or your temperature spikes, I'm taking you to the doctor."

"Got it," I replied, smiling inside.

Before Henry dropped me off home, he pulled into McDonald's and ordered me a Big Mac and fries. Usually, eating fast food would be a big no, but he was really trying to make me happy. Apart from that terrible night at the beach, I was content living here.

We rolled up to the house by the curb, but Henry left the truck idling. He turned to me as he leaned over the steering wheel and said, "I gotta get back to work unless you need me to stay home. I can call my partner to fill in for me."

"Dad, no. Go to work. I'm not a little kid anymore. I'm a senior in high school. If I need you, I'll call. Don't worry. Grandpa should be home shortly."

Henry's lips thinned into a frown. "Please call me if you need anything and stay in the house with the door locked. Don't answer the door to anyone unless it's your friend, Candy. He can come over, but only for a short while. Don't worry about dinner tonight. I'll pick up something at the market. I should be home early. When it rains, we can't do much building."

"Dad, you worry too much." I hugged him and scooted out the door and ran to the front porch for cover. Henry waited until he saw me closing the door. Judging by his long face, he didn't like the idea of leaving me alone. No point in him staying home. I knew how to take my temperature and heat Campbell's Soup.

The house was drafty and smelled of burnt apples. Last night, Grandpa baked an apple pie and forgot to set the timer. By the time he remembered, smoke had filled the kitchen, and the pie had burnt to a solid black crisp.

I turned the furnace up and headed upstairs to my loft with my McDonalds. As I climbed the stairs, the rain pounded the roof like millions of tiny hammers. I didn't mind the noise. I loved the attic. My favorite was the number of windows. I had a view at every angle, but today the tar-blacked clouds cast shadows in all the cracks and nooks of the house, leaving the rooms lifeless.

Flopping down on my squeaky bed, I crossed my legs, sitting in the center. I flipped on the lamp on the nightstand and grabbed my earbuds then plugged them into my phone. I held my breath, fretting my phone might still be waterlogged. I turned the volume up, and music began to flow. Mirth touched my lips as I started humming to *Foster the People*. Great artist.

My eyes dropped to my burger as I peeled the wrapper away. The anticipation overwhelmed me as my mouth watered for that special sauce. I chomped down on the insane burger, savoring all the juices. I closed my eyes, listening to the fast rhythm of the song while chewing.

Then something unexpected happened. My stomach lurched as my body rejected the food. I leaped off the bed and dove for the toilet, barely making it in time to purge my entire guts out. When I had nothing else to expel, I slid down to the cold tile floor into a fetal position and rode out the sharp ache. I moaned, squeezing my eyes tight, gripping my stomach. The insufferable pain consumed me.

When my eyes fluttered open, I heard feet scuffing across the floor. Henry or Grandpa must be home. Stretched out across my bed, I realized someone had moved me. I must've been unconscious for a few hours. Darkness veiled my room with only a soft glow from the string of lights that hovered above me. I rose on my elbows and called out, "Dad!" I raked my eyes over my room and waited to hear his heavy boots tromping up the stairs.

Startled, I caught a glimpse of a shadow stirring from the far corner of my room. I gasped as I rushed to sit up. Then I heard a deep male's voice pierce the shadows. "Ah, she awakes." Valentine slowly stepped into the faint light.

"How did you get in here? I locked my door," I grumbled as a sharp pain struck. I clenched my stomach, bitting out the wave. "I want my dad," I demanded breathlessly.

"Your father is working late, and your friend, Candy, is home cooking a feast for his mother."

"How do you know these things?" I squeezed down once again, bearing the misery. "What time is it?"

"Ten-ish. I think." His gentle voice drifted in the air as he eased down on the edge of my bed.

"What is wrong with me?"

Valentine tucked a strand of hair behind my ear and spoke. "Your vital organs are shutting down. That's why your body is rejecting mortal food. Just like I said, your body is changing. Soon, you will have to cross. I'm near my end as I cling to my last bit of humanity, but it is a losing battle. Soon, I will have to feed."

"Change? Cross? Feed? Stop talking in riddles and tell me already!" I screeched.

"What happened to you wasn't a school-kid prank. The drink you ingested was the blood of a vampire." There was a faint tremor in his voice as though some emotion had touched him. He continued, "A very powerful sire that has chosen you to be Diablo's mate."

"I will never agree to such absurdity!"

"Micki, it doesn't matter what you want. You have no choice."

"Why me?" I choked out.

"Diablo's been restless and growing more dangerous than the norm. Our sire decided to give you to him. He thinks you would make Diablo happy."

Anger struck me like a white-hot branding iron. "That's disgusting," I snarled. "I'll never agree to such barbarity. Who is this sire, anyway?"

"You don't get a choice. And you can't speak to the sire. He remains hidden. No one has ever seen him."

Fed up, I shoved Valentine off my bed. "Get out! I don't believe you. Leave!"

He rose in one fluid motion, looming over me, his eyes stone-cold. "No matter how much you deny this, the fact remains that my brother views you as his gift." He pulled me roughly, almost violently to him. "Don't you understand? Diablo is a sadistic vampire. He will take you against your will."

"I'm calling the police!" I jerked from his clenches.

"Call!" he challenged, throwing his arms in the air. "A whole platoon couldn't stop me and especially Diablo."

"If I'm so doomed, then why bother. I mean... don't you have someone else to nag?" I lifted my chin, meeting his icy gaze straight on.

"Don't you get it? I don't want Diablo anywhere near you!" Valentine bit out between his teeth.

"Don't worry. That creep isn't touching me."

"Don't underestimate my brother."

"This is all one sick joke that you and Wendy and her stupid minions have conjured up." I waved my hand over his frame. "If you were dead, you wouldn't be standing in the middle of my bedroom."

"I'm not joking."

"Okay, humor me. How did you become... *dead*?"

"Diablo found me and fed me the same drink from the same bottle."

"Is he your sire?" I couldn't believe I was entertaining this.

"No. He's the leader of our coven. We call ourselves *The Sons of Blood*." Valentine sauntered to the window by the bed and stared out, keeping his back to me. "A sire is pure, and only they can turn a human."

"When you say turn, you mean..."

"A vampire."

A sudden thin chill hung on the edge of his words, but I still refused to believe him. "You're crazy."

"If I'm insane, then explain to me what is happening to you?"

"I have a virus. A bug. I'll sleep it off and be fine tomorrow." I was trying to convince myself more than him.

"Keep telling yourself that, sweetheart." He lunged at me but vanished before he reached my side. Gone. Vanquished from sight.

I sat there stunned, frozen, my eyes blinking at the vacant shadows. My attention was jarred when I heard Henry's voice. Struck with a sudden bout of relief, I leaped to my feet and ran downstairs, throwing myself into Henry's embrace. He stumbled back and hugged me. Then he held me at arm's length with a dumbfounded look across his face. "Is everything all right?" He laid his palm over my forehead. "You're not running a fever. You're sorta cool."

I wiped the moisture from my eyes. "I'm better and happy you're home."

"Mick, I'm really starting to get concerned about you." He hung his coat on the rack and turned back to me. "You feel up to eating?"

Then the burger from earlier came to mind, and my stomach roiled. "No, I'm fine. That burger did the trick, Dad." I smiled, fearing he could see through my farce.

"All right. I stopped and got us some barbeque, but I think I'll put it in the fridge and have a can of Campbell's soup and hit the bed. Long day," he smiled, messing my hair up. I laughed, swatting his hand away and pulling the strands out of my face. "Did Grandpa make it home?" Henry asked.

"Nope. He's probably staying the night with his lady friend, Ms. Betty."

Henry chuckled, "Grandpa is almost seventy and has more girlfriends than a teenage boy." He shook his head. "There should be something wrong with that."

"Goodnight, Dad. I'm heading back to bed."

"See you in the morn, jellybean. Sorry for getting home late."

"It's okay. I'm a big girl now." I lifted up on my toes and gave Henry a peck on the cheek before trotting upstairs.

Before I climbed into bed, I checked my windows. It puzzled me how Valentine had gotten into the house or how he vanished before my eyes so abruptly, but I'd sleep a little better knowing my windows were locked. Though, I suspected a little old lock wouldn't keep him out.

# Foes and Friends

"Gul, I can't believe you went down to that park alone." Candy stared at me in shock as he bounced with the bumpy rhythm of the school bus. "I'm sorry I didn't check on you. Man, I made a D in history, and Mama grounded me from my phone and goin' anywhere."

"It's okay. My decision was hasty and stupid, but I didn't want to involve you any more than I have already."

"Did the mofo pony up?" Candy pursed his lips.

I grimaced. "No. Not really. When Valentine snuck into my house..."

"Shut the door!" His deep green eyes gleamed with alarm. "That mofo broke into your house? For real?"

"Yeah, and the strangest part, there were no signs of a break-in. The security alarm didn't go off, either."

"That's crazy!" He stared at me in shock.

"You're telling me," I answered, feeling vulnerable.

"You got to tell your Dad that you've got a serious stalker problem."

"Some would beg to differ. I trailed after Valentine at the park."

"The park is public. Your mofo house ain't," Candy argued.

"True. But I got 'em stirred."

The bus pulled into the school and rolled to a halt. The hydraulic brakes swished as the driver cut the motor and slid the lever, opening the doors. Students piled in line as they exited.

When Candy and I meandered through the side entrance, he asked, "You got a costume yet? The town's Halloween Carnival is tomorrow."

"Yeah, I got an idea I'm working. What about you?"

"I'm gonna go as a drag queen."

"You're supposed to wear a costume, dude." I nudged his shoulder, giggling.

"Oh, hush your mouth."

Throwing my arm over his shoulder and drawing him near, I said, "We should both go as drag queens."

"We gonna have a fais do-do," Candy flashed his white teeth.

"What does that mean?" I swore Louisiana had the weirdest lingo.

"It means we gonna party." Candy high-fived me.

Straight up noon, the halls roared of hungry students. I met up with Candy at the gym. We walked to the cafeteria together, falling in behind the crowd.

With our trays full, Candy and I edged our way through the chattering cafeteria to our favorite spot next to the far window. It was usually just the two of us. Two unconventional friends that complimented each other's nonconformity to what society had deemed as normal. Candy and his artistic flair and my obsession with wearing black. I liked our oddness.

Most of the students here had formed bonds since kindergarten. Then you have the favorite students... *the popular.* I never understood the reasoning behind that theory. Popular meant well-liked. But in all honesty, they were the mean kids. Stuck-up snobs.

After settling at our table, I kicked off the conversation. "Hey, you got a dress I can borrow?"

"Hold on there! You expect me to provide your Halloween costume?" Candy pursed his lips.

"Uh, yeah. I need some of your makeup too."

"Boo, you do know I'm black?"

I rolled my eyes. "Duh! I meant your blush and eye shadow. We can stop off at your beauty salon, Dark and Lovely, where you buy your makeup, and I can buy my own."

"I don't think they have your shade. The salon works on black folks' hair." His brows knitted. "You're like baby powder white."

"I am not!" I rebutted. "I can go dark, and we could be twins."

"Oh, hell, no! You can't look this good," he pouted, waving his hands over his body.

"I'm one up on you, dude. I have boobs."

"Do you always have to be tacky?" Candy fanned his flushed face.

When I started to reply to Candy's remark, my eyes landed on Wendy standing beside me, feigning a broad smile. My pulse sped up a few notches as our eyes hitched.

"Hello there!" Wendy sang far sweeter than her usual. Without bothering to ask, she helped herself to a chair at our table.

My eyes cut directly at her. "What do you want?"

"Do I have to have a reason to come sit with y'all?" There was deceit behind her glint. My defenses sounded off immediately.

Candy's curt voice lashed out at our unwanted company. "Chile, the air you breathe is wicked. Bye, girl!" He swatted at her like a fly.

She cut her black eyes at him as if she wanted to slash his throat. "I'm not talking to you." She then focused her dark eyes at me. "Several of us are having a circle tonight. You should come." She slipped Candy a sneer. "You can bring your sidekick if you wish."

"Are you insane?" I gaped at her.

"I understand if you don't trust me, but this is a special night, blessing the harvest. It's all very harmless. Aren't you a witch anyway? You look the part." Her dark eyes roamed over my attire.

"My wearing black doesn't mean I worship the devil." Irritation glided off my tongue.

"Wicca has nothing to do with the devil," she paused. "I might add that Valentine will be there." Wendy obviously thought I'd jump at the chance to see him. She might be right.

"Why do you think I care? He's *your* friend, not mine." I narrowed my eyes at her assumption.

"I see that he has taken you under his wing. And you are always looking for him. Naturally, I would assume that you two are becoming... *friends.*"

I asked with mild curiosity. "Where and when?"

"I'm holding the ceremony at the old Eastwick barn, a few miles outside the city limits. Ask anyone. They can tell you the directions. Tonight, ten o'clock sharp."

"I don't know." I tossed a bold smile, wishing I had stones to throw instead.

"Setting aside our differences, I'd like to make it up to you. I hope you will come." Wendy slid out of her chair as her pink skirt ruffled like petticoats. A smile found its way to her lips. "I look forward to seeing you both." Without another word, Wendy twirled on her high heels, swaying her hips back and forth like a cheap hooker heading to the usual street corner.

"Yeah, not if we see you first." Candy popped off, mumbling under his breath.

"I don't have a good feeling about this. It's a school night anyway. Doubt my dad will let me go."

"Don't you know how to climb out your bedroom window?"

"What if it's another setup?" Alarm struck me like a baseball bat to the head.

"Valentine will be there, and if we go, I'll bring my mama's gris-gris." Candy insisted.

"What is that?" I asked.

"It's a small pouch of lucky charms. It wards off bad juju."

"Do you really believe in all that hocus pocus?" I laughed, a little freaked out.

"I sure do. Anyhoo, what can it hurt?"

"Nothing, I guess." I glanced down at my burrito as my stomach suddenly roiled. I shoved it to the side. Lately, food hasn't been agreeable. Not even cereal and I loved my corn flakes.

Valentine came to mind... *and his claim of how my body was shutting down.* I scoffed to myself. His farfetched story was just that, yet I was frightened. There was a ring of truth to what he said. Though, a large part of me wanted to shelve it as a fairy tale. All the more reason to speak to him. If I had a chance to catch Valentine alone, the barn might be perfect.

Apart from sneaking out, I wasn't sure how we'd get there. Neither Candy or I owned a car, and I doubted a taxi would go outside the city limits. Even if a cab drove that far out, where would we get the DOE-RAY-ME? "What's the point? Unless I find a magical broomstick for us to ride." I toyed with the straw in my Coke.

"Maybe my cousin, Dwight, can take us," Candy suggested.

"You have a cousin with a car?"

"Boo, half the town here is kin to me."

"It must be nice. It's only my dad and grandpa." A prick of loneliness struck my heart. Having a cousin to chill with might've been fun.

"You don't have a sister or a brother?" he asked.

"Nope. My parents never got around to their second child. Then Mom had an affair and left," I frowned.

"Hold up! Your mom messed around on your pop?"

"Yep. My mom married her boss. I had to live with them for a while. I hate my stepfather, Phil. He's filthy rich, and a bully."

"You rich?" Candy looked at me as if he'd seen me for the first time.

"My stepfather is wealthy. I'd rather drink poison than take any of his money."

"Man! Sorry to hear that." Candy's face dropped.

"What about you? You got a brother or...?"

"My brother, Troy, is a marine. We don't get to see him much. He's deployed in Afghanistan. We only get to hear from him once a month, but Mom and I get to send him emails, and he replies when he can." Candy paused, taking a heavy breath. "I miss my brother. He knew I was gay before I did. He didn't rat on me with Mama either. Troy and I were tight. Nobody messed with me when he was around." Candy looked away for a moment, a little misty-eyed.

"How long has he been gone?" My heart ached for my friend.

"A year. We're hoping Troy gets to come home in a few months."

I smiled, reaching for his hand. "What a happy day that will be."

"Dang, straight!" Candy wiped his nose with his sleeve.

"Enough about family," I winked. "Talk to your cousin."

"I'm on it." Candy pulled out his phone from his jean pocket and punched the numbers.

* * *

That night at dinner, I made a pot of gumbo. I found the recipe online and a good thing too. I had no idea where to start.

I figured if I finished my homework and straightened up the house, plus cooked a tasty meal, Henry might let me go out for a couple of hours tonight. Sneaking out had its perks, but I didn't want to rock the boat with my newfound freedom.

Come dinner time, we gathered at the table with Henry hiding behind the newspaper and Grandpa listening to his staticky radio. The static hum drifted throughout the house, getting on my last nerve. What unfortunate luck that a fifty-year-old radio still played and only *A.M.* I internally crossed my eyes.

Time to focus. I sat up straight and cleared my throat. "Dad," I said as Henry popped his head out from under the paper and rested his eyes on me. Good! I'd gotten his attention now. "A few kids from school are having a barn party. It's a Halloween thing," I swallowed. "Anyway, Candy and I are invited."

"Tomorrow night?" A dark brow arched above the paper.

"No. The carnival is tomorrow. These are kids from school. They do it every year. Uh… Candy's going," I quickly added.

"Where's this barn at?" Henry took a sip of his tea.

"On Eastwick Road."

"I'm familiar with the place. Eastwick barn has been around for more than a century." Then he wrinkled his nose and asked, "I thought you said you didn't have any friends other than Candy."

"Quit drillin' the lassie, son. Let the girl live," Grandpa interjected.

"Pop, I got this, please." Irritation ruffled Henry's voice.

My eyes bounced between Grandpa and Henry. Then I furthered with my spiel. "Hmm, I'm starting to make friends," I smiled tentatively.

"I'm glad you're starting to give this place a chance. Friends help." Henry's face grew into a broad grin.

"Lassie, I can take you and that young lad if you like," Grandpa offered.

I wrinkled my nose, "Grandpa, I appreciate it but not in the El Camino," I laughed. "I want to make friends, not run them off."

"Aye, Lassie, I thought you liked me car."

"Grandpa, that was when I was five." I sunk down into my seat.

"Don't worry, jellybean. Grandpa plans to finish up his knitting tonight." Henry glanced over at Grandpa. "Aren't you making me a sweater, Pops?"

"Aye, I guess I'm held to prior arrangements. Sorry, Lassie," Grandpa winked.

"It's okay, Grandpa," I smiled, but grateful I got outta that ride. "So, can I go?" I looked back at Henry.

"Mick, it's a school night. You know the rules." Henry sounded firm, not budging an inch.

"I know Dad, but this is a special night, and it's Halloween."

"Halloween isn't officially until tomorrow." Henry raised a pointy brow.

"I promise I'll be back by midnight. Candy has to be back home too."

Henry chuckled as his eyes combed the dining room. "That explains the clean house and a cooked meal."

I smiled into my bowl.

"All right. You have to be home, not a minute past eleven. Not a minute later."

I sprung to my feet and threw my arms around Henry. "Thanks, Dad!" I kissed him on the cheek.

He patted my hand and said, "I want you calling me when you get there. Keep your phone on you at all times."

"Okay, I promise." I kissed him again on the cheek and rushed upstairs to grab my purse.

Moments later, I pounded on Candy's door. He answered after two knocks. "I thought your dad wasn't gonna let you go."

"Me too!" I stepped inside. "Where's your mama?"

"She's workin' late," he shrugged.

"Wow! Ms. Candy works as much as my dad."

"It's cool, yonno."

"Hey, is your cousin picking us up?"

"I got something better." Candy pulled out a key from his pocket and dangled it in front of me. "He loaned me his car with a full tank." His lips spread into a broad smile; straight white teeth sparkled.

"Wow! What a nice cousin." I almost jumped with joy.

"Trust me. It's gonna cost me."

"Candy, you're not doing anything illegal or …." My chin dropped to the floor.

"No, man! I gotta wash his car a thousand and one times." He pursed his lips. "You thought I was gonna deal drugs?" He stared at me. His aura turned a sickly mustard color. I knew then I'd hurt his feelings, and guilt squeezed my chest.

"Look, I'm sorry. I have no room to talk," I sighed. "I didn't tell you this because I didn't want you to think bad of me, but I got busted for pot. Two measly joints. The one good thing my stepfather ever did for me was getting the charges reduced to a misdemeanor. The police were charging me with the intent to distribute. It scared me so much. I thought my life was ruined forever and the worse part… the pot wasn't even mine. I was wearing my friend's jacket. It was in the pocket where she left them in a hidden compartment. That night my friend went home, and I got carted off to jail." I swallowed the pain in my throat.

"Damn, gul. Misery loves you."

"Don't I know it!" I huffed out a long breath. "So, you're gonna have dish-pan hands for a bit?" I threw in a little humor to blot out the heavy.

"Don't jerk my string. That crap ain't funny." Candy shook his head, probably counting how many times he'd have to wash his cousin's car.

"I'm in this deal too. You're not the only one that gets all the fun. I'll be helping you for the next several months," I smiled, nudging him in the stomach with my elbow.

"You'd help me?"

"Why wouldn't I. I got you in this mess."

"Dang! You are just full of surprises." His eyes brightened. "Let's get this over with. I got House-wives recorded."

"Yeah, you're definitely gay, dude," I laughed.

"Shut up! Straight men watch that show too."

"Straight men in the closet," I teased.

"Whatever!" He pouted as we headed outside. Candy slid into the driver's seat, and I took the passenger's side.

"Will this old Lincoln run? I mean, this car has gotta be more than thirty years old." My eyes washed over the black interior. It was spotless, a shiny dash, clean carpet, and had a pair of cloth dice hanging over the mirror. A bit cheesy but cute.

"It's a classic seventy-five. It'll get us there. I can't say f'sure about the return," he shrugged dismissively, eyeing the dashboard.

"Yeah, you may be right about that." I agreed as we both burst into laughter.

# The Circle

The tires crunched against the gravel as we rolled down Eastwick Road. Looming oaks with spidey-like baskets nestled in its branches enshrouded us with eerie shadows.

After a couple of miles down the winding path, we came to a break in the dense tree line to an open field. The full moon hung like a luminous pearl shedding its silvery light on a large dilapidated building amid the meadow.

I nodded in its direction. "I'm guessing that's the famous barn." The building embosomed a ghostly presence, sitting alone. No doubt it'd seen better days. The red paint had faded, revealing gray boards. At the south end, it drooped to one side as if it had sunk five feet into the soil.

"Yup. This place is spooky as heck durin' the day. It's ten times worse at night." Candy shifted in his seat, nervously.

"No lie," I scoffed. I understood why Wendy picked this place. I envisioned people gathered around a crystal ball having a séance. Unexpectedly, a chill slithered through me.

"The Eastwick barn has been around for centuries. Like it's frozen in time. Never changing. You'd think it would collapse into splinters after all these years." Candy sat there a moment, chewing on his lip, staring at it.

"It's breath-taking," I whispered, unable to peel my eyes away.

"Whatever you do, don't blow on it."

"Don't worry." I gave a curt laugh, but inside, my stomach swirled with fret.

We pulled behind a long line of cars parked off the road onto a stretch of wild butterweed. I spotted Valentine's Harley across the field parked by the barn. Its chrome glinted in the moonlight as if it were glowing. Sudden relief clenched my heart. He came.

On the other hand, breathing the same air with wicked Wendy and her menacing duo gave me pause. If I lowered my guard for a split second, I might end up with a knife in my back. This time, I intended to proceed with a mountain of caution.

Jarring my attention back, Candy cut the engine and pulled the key from the ignition, sighing out loud. He gave me a sidelong glance. "You sure you wanna do this?"

"I'm not sure about anything." My eyes fixated on the old dwelling. Between sneezing from the hay and the smell of manure and then all the sharp tools that hung from the beams, I questioned my decision. "It'd take only a flick of a cigarette, and we'd go up in a flame of glory."

"You is killin' my party buzz." Candy cut his eyes at me. "Man up! If my skinny butt can march in there like I own the place, so can you." Despite his attempt at bravery, the trepidation in his voice sang loud and clear. Maybe he was onto something. Maybe I should not be so foolish.

"We can turn this car around and go home. No one will notice our absence." Setting aside my disdain for Wendy and this place, my desire to speak with Valentine pestered me like sand in my shorts. I'd admit, seeing Valentine wasn't just about my pending problem. He intrigued me. I supposed I saw something different in him. The kindness in his eyes, his angelic face, always on the verge of a smile, his golden wheat hair, his towering height and last but not least... the mystery that clung to him like static electricity. He defied the rules and owned an air of arrogance. Yet, these traits did not define him at all.

Then I remembered that raunchy gang he called *The Sons of Blood*. And because of his poor choice of *BFFs*, I didn't foresee us as close friends.

"Let's go get a burger and go home." Candy suggested as if he'd read my mind.

"That sounds like a great idea. I know the perfect place downtown."

When Candy turned the key to start the engine, the car stalled. "This can't be happenin'." He tried it again, pumping the gas, but to no avail. Only muffled sounds of a constant clicking blended with the night's hum.

I touched his shoulder and spoke softly. "Maybe give it a rest for a minute. The engine is flooded."

"What the...," he cursed under his breath. "This is all your fault. You practically twisted my arm!"

"I did no such thing!" I screeched. "It was your idea to borrow your cousin's junk-car!" I couldn't believe my best friend blamed me. Then I reminded myself why he came in the first place. I blew out a sharp breath. "Hey, I'm sorry. I forget why you're here." I bit my bottom lip, smiling. "Why don't I call my dad?"

"Sorry for blowin' up at you too." Remorse coated his voice. "But call your papa so we can get the mofo outta 'ere!" Candy plucked my purse from the back-seat and tossed it in my lap.

"Good idea!" I started digging in my bag and came to a hallowing realization. "Crap!" My eyes snapped up at Candy. "I forgot my phone!" Then it dawned on me... "Hey, I can call him from yours."

"You gotta be kiddin' me!" Candy sat straight up in his seat, running his palm over his mouth. "My phone service got cut off today. Mama couldn't pay the bill this month. We've been eatin' nothin' but taters."

"A minute ago, we were gonna go eat burgers. You had money, then."

"I was hopin' you'd pay. I did get the wheels, yonno." He arched a brow.

"The wheels are fabulous, but the car's a lemon."

"This turned out to be a crappy night. Now we gotta walk." He leaned his head back, rubbing his eyes.

"Candy, why didn't you tell me, you and your mom were having problems?"

"Boo, we live in the hood. Everybody's got troubles."

"Does your mom know anything about carpentry?"

"My mama fixes everything around the house. There ain't nothin' she can't do," Candy boasted. His slight tilt in his chin showed his pride in his mom.

"I'll talk to Dad." Awkwardly, I cleared my throat. "Let's do this." I opened my door and stepped out onto the weeds, accompanying Candy by his side. "If we stick together, nothing will happen," I swore. Though I doubted my own words.

"All right. But if I see a mofo ghost, I'm leavin' you where you stand." Candy fussed as he slid out of the car and slammed the door a bit too hard.

"Copy that," I smiled, swinging my arm over his shoulder.

We followed the path of trodden ironweed, crunching twigs underfoot. I noticed a soft, gold light flickering in one of the windows. Or maybe it was a half door to a stall? Nonetheless, my heart leaped in my throat. "Great! They have candles burning in an old, wooden barn filled with dry hay. Really smart."

"You kiddin' me?" Candy's voice shot up an octave. "My knees are already knockin' gul." Candy clutched my arm tighter, leaning on me.

"I'm sure I can borrow someone's phone." I attempted to convince myself as much as Candy. Even still, I sensed alarm, stirring my blood to unrest. "Let's relax and have a little fun." My eyes roamed over the silver cast field as a faint breeze tousled the white flowers. Though this place was inundated with creepy, I admired its raw beauty.

"I'm gonna age before my time if we keep doin' this spooky crap." Candy pressed his lips together.

"No argument from me," I giggled. Candy could make the worst situation comical.

Arm in arm, we emerged in the clearing. Aimless laughter drifted from the barn. As we neared, my heart leaped into my throat. Too late to back out now.

We paused at the threshold of the barn before entering. Endless tittering spilled over into the vast space as shadows danced among the throng of black-robed guests, huddled in the center of the barn. Hay swathed the planks, making my nose itch and eyes water. I spotted about five half-door stalls, no sign of livestock, though.

A wave of alarm struck when my eyes halted on the farming tools at the far left corner. I began ticking off the devices, a sharp pointy pitchfork, an ax, some sorta plow blade, maybe an attachment to a tractor along with other sharp objects swinging on hooks. Pointy objects gave me the heebie-jeebies. A good enough excuse for Candy and me to split. Maybe I'd made a mistake letting Wendy lure us here. Jesus! This Halloween fest better not be a lynching. My eyes bounced between the black robes. I didn't recognize anyone from school. These folks were too old to be high-schoolers.

Candy and I shared a strained glance before we stepped inside to join the guests. It was daunting to approach a small crowd of faceless people hiding underneath their hoods.

I fiddled with a strand of hair, feeling out of sorts as several shadowed eyes turned on Candy and me. Strangely, I didn't sense trouble. I saw several auras, various yellows, gold, and pastel. Optimistic and easy-going people usually carried these colors.

On the downside, we still had to factor in the unpredictability of wicked Wendy. I would rather trust a python than her. As soon as I snagged Valentine and had my chat with him, I planned to leave and not a minute later. Of course, that depended on borrowing someone's phone to call Henry.

Candy glanced restlessly over his shoulder. "Can we leave now?"

"Our car won't start. Remember?" I whispered back.

"Mother...!" he huffed curses under his breath. "Remind me to whoop the daylights outta my cousin if we make it back alive."

"Why your cousin?" my brows furrowed.

"Cuss, if he hadn't said yes, we'd be home watchin' Andy Cohen and eatin' popcorn."

Candy and his silly reasoning. "We're about to enter a witch's circle, and you want to smack your cousin?" I shook my head, laughing. "Well, we're here. Let's go mingle."

We trekked our way to greet the guests when Wendy popped up beside us. I noticed she held something behind her back. Suspicion trickled down my spine.

"Glad you decided to come." Wendy's cherry-red lips overshadowed her heart-shaped face. Quite delicate features to wear such a bold lipstick.

"Why the robes?" I nodded over at the guests.

"Tonight is Mabon," Wendy smiled. "It's one of the Wiccan sabbats. It is an important celebration. Every year, on the Autumn Equinox, we join in a circle to celebrate the harvest."

At that moment, silence smothered the thick air. Candy and I shared a pinched glance. I wondered how many folks in Eastwick practiced Wicca. Louisiana contained more than its fair share of peculiarity.

Wendy forged on, ignoring our wide eyes. "We pay our respects to the impending dark and give thanks to the waning light. This is an ancient tradition handed down over many generations. Every year on Mabon, we gather in a circle to celebrate growth. We honor this celebration by partaking, right before, Samhain."

"What is Samhain?" I asked, brows knitted.

"It's Halloween," Wendy clarified.

Suddenly Candy blurted out, "I knew it! You're a mofo witch." He bounced on his feet like he'd won the million-dollar lottery.

"I am a witch." She divulged matter-of-factly.

Candy eyed her skeptically. "That's devil-worshiping, right?"

"Wicca is pure magick. We celebrate nature. Samhain is a time to remember people in our lives who have passed away. We celebrate the dead. Anyway, I am glad you came. We always can use new members in our circle."

"Hmm, I appreciate the offer, but since we're underdressed for the celebration, Candy and I will sit this one out." I bestowed a snarky smile as I crossed my arms over my chest. I had no intention of joining this gang any more than the last one she introduced me to.

"Oh, no! I insist. I have robes for both of you." She held up two folded black robes and nodded toward the south end of the barn. "There's a room in the back where you can change."

My eyes widened. "Uh… that's nice of you to consider us, but we're having car trouble. If I could borrow your phone to call my dad, we'll be on our way."

"Don't be silly," Wendy flashed a bright smile. "The ceremony won't take long. Afterward, you can make your call."

I glanced at the black capes and shook my head. "Thanks, but no thanks. We're not participating."

"Of course, you are," she insisted. "We mustn't anger the Goddess, now must we?" I sensed a sneaky scheme behind her sweet-buttery pretense.

Hating that I had to play nice, I realized it would be in our best interest to appease Wendy. What other choice did we have? Walk twenty miles? I slid my gaze at Candy and then cut my eyes back at Wendy, snatching the two folded robes from her grasp. I feigned a honeydew smile and nodded for Candy to follow me.

"Oh, I almost forgot," Wendy called out.

What now? I halted, tossing a glance over my shoulder, biting down my ire. "Yes," I huffed.

A wide smile broke across her porcelain face. "You can't wear any clothing under your robe. Nudity is part of opening yourself to nature." And there went the corn syrup smile.

Candy's eyes nearly popped out of his head as I stood there, startled. This was getting worse by the minute. I snapped my mouth shut and composed myself, adding a little sass. "No problem. I go naked under my clothing all the time." I turned on my heels, grabbing Candy's hand, pulling him with me to the dressing room.

We entered through a door into a dark room with a profound smell of mold and dry straw. Judging by the age of this barn, I searched for the chain to the ceiling light. Lucky for us, a shaft of moonlight filtered through the small window. I caught a glimmer of a silver string hanging in the center of the space. I wrapped my fingers around the thin metal and tugged. A quick click and a dim light showered the room. Talk about tight. My eyes brushed over the space. More like a closet, nothing short of a ten by ten.

"I guess we can undress with our backs to each other." Not something I intended, undressing in front of a boy for the first time. Talk about awkward. I'd never experienced as much as a kiss. Boys asked me out, but after spending five minutes with one, I'd lose interest. I liked boys, and I always appreciated ogling over the next hot guy, but when they showed their ignorance, it killed the mood for me.

"I told you she was a witch!"

"Shush! She'll hear you." I cracked the door open to peek out. I looked back at Candy. "I think it's safe."

"I am not taking my lucky drawers off for anyone! Wendy can't make me either."

"Your drawers can't be that lucky. Look where we're at!"

"Tacky, much? Turn your lily-white self around. Let's get this over with." Candy blew out in a heated rush. "I wanna go home and watch my shows."

"That's music to my ears, dude." I turned my back to him and started peeling off my clothing. "Sorry for dragging you into this," I spoke with my back to him.

"Yeah, me too. But I would've come anyway. Can't have you tracing off alone with those psycho witches."

"You can be really sweet when you want to." My eyes moistened.

"Stop gettin' mushy. Just get dressed," Candy grumbled.

"Whatever!" I sniffled, laughing to myself.

With a long sigh of regret, Candy and I found ourselves in the mix of the guests. We clung to each other for support, carefully keeping our eyes down. I think our pounding hearts were in sync as we stood locked arm in arm.

A quick glimpse caught my attention when my eyes met Valentine's face, dressed in a black robe like the rest of the guests. He stood there devilishly handsome. He towered over the other men by a full eight inches. When our eyes pierced the distance between us, I felt a ripple of excitement wash over me. I was more than just grateful for Valentine's presence. I was elated. I suddenly liked having his attention. Although he might not be pleased with me. He'd warned me to stay away from Wendy.

Jarring my thoughts, Wendy hopped up on a stack of hay and shouted. "It's time! Come gather." Alarm squeezed my stomach. I shared an unquiet glance with Candy. His frightful eyes mirrored mine. We both questioned if we'd been too hasty coming here tonight.

Candy and I drew closer as Wendy waved her hands in a circular motion. "It's time, everyone. Only moments before midnight." Wendy jumped off the hay and gestured for all thirteen of us to form a circle. Wendy took a box of salt and sprinkled it all around each one's feet.

"With salt, I cleanse," she called out, stretching her arms apart. "Everyone, join hands." Self-consciousness startled me. I had no idea what to expect. I swapped a glance at Valentine. Seeing his quietude, it settled my nerves but not entirely.

A bearded man on my left reached to take my hand. I paused for a second, eyeing the guests as they formed a circle. Squinching internally, I took his rough-palmed hand. The grubby old man's fingernails looked like he hadn't washed his hands in a week. I reminded myself that I saw a bathroom in the back. Candy clasped my right hand and the hand of a young Asian girl on his right.

As I waited in silence, it dawned on me that I hadn't seen Wendy's sidekicks, Ella, and Cindy. I wondered if they ran out of glue. I'd assumed Wendy never left the house without the mindless duo, and I didn't see Diablo and his partner, Romeo. I was grateful for that little peace of mind.

Wendy lifted her arms up to the sky as we followed her lead. She called out, "I give thanks to the Goddess!" And then the circle repeated her words. Too weirded out to speak, I popped my mouth open but then shut it quickly. Candy followed along better than I did. I shot him a quick smile. I figured he knew more about magick and tradition since he'd lived in this backward state all his life.

"Today the sun enters Libra, the balance," Wendy paused, raising her voice. "Today, we give thanks to Mother Earth and celebrate the harvest she has bestowed upon us."

The circle called out into the night air. "Blessed be!"

Candy and I shared a giggle.

"As we gather our harvest, the season blesses us with plenty," Wendy sang.

The circle repeated, "Blessed be."

"Okay, y'all! Join hands and move counterclockwise," Wendy instructed. As we moved, voices rose high. "We are grateful for the bounty we've received. Blessed be." Everyone repeated the chorus over and over as we danced in a circle.

I mumbled the words along with the rest. In a weird eerie way, this reminded me back when I was a kid at the skating rink dancing to the hokey-pokey.

All at once, electricity in the air hissed as the chanting grew with intensity. I quickly kept in step, round and round, faster and faster as if my legs had taken flight, and I was floating to the stars. I held my eyes closed tight; a flurry of feelings bubbled up, giddy, dazed and confused.

When the chanting ended, I lost my footing, crashing to the floor. My eyes fluttered open, and two worried violet eyes came into focus. "*Valentine!*" I softly whispered. He was kneeling over me, holding me halfway in his arms. I noticed several pairs of eyes peering over his broad shoulder. I jolted up, pulling from his embrace. "What happened?" I touched my throbbing forehead.

"You fainted." Valentine's silky voice pierced the fog in my head. He held out his hand to assist me to my feet.

"Uh... thank you," I mumbled, taking his hand. Once I balanced myself, standing on two feet, I dropped his hand, feeling the burn of my heated cheeks. "Hmm, where is Candy?"

Candy pushed past a couple of tall men and rushed to my side. "Here I am."

"We need to get home," I said and then turned to Valentine. "Do you know anything about cars?"

He scratched behind his ear and appeared to be on the edge of a laugh as if he had a private joke. "I've worked on a few motors."

"Our car stalled. Can you take a look?" I asked, sensing every eye here was staring at us.

"Sure." He flashed a lopsided grin. "Lead the way." Valentine gestured.

"Let Candy and I slip back into our clothes first."

"No problem. I'll meet you back here. I guess I can change too," Valentine smiled as he scratched his day-old stubble.

"Sure." I smiled back and then grabbed Candy's arm, heading for the dressing room. "See you in a minute." I tossed over my shoulder.

Candy whispered in my ear. "Boo, he likes you."

I snorted, "No, he doesn't."

"Uh, huh. You keep tellin' yourself that."

"Shush! He'll hear you," I mumbled under my breath, attempting to keep my blush to a mild pink.

When the three of us reached the car, Valentine didn't waste any time. "Hey, brother, lift the hood." Then he turned to me and asked, "You can hold the flashlight," he smiled as he handed it to me.

Candy jumped in the driver's seat and popped the hood. He sat in the car waiting for Valentine to instruct him on the next move.

I held the flashlight over the engine. I was grateful that Valentine had one handy. Ominous clouds had swallowed up the moon and stars, leaving us under a dark cast.

I crossed my fingers, hoping that Valentine got the car running soon. Calling Henry at this late hour would mean the end of my short-lived freedom. It was already past midnight.

I watched in silence as Valentine leaned under the hood. While his lower body hung out, I ogled in silence, holding my breath as he tinkered with the engine. Minutes later, he stuck his head out and shouted to Candy. "Crank it up."

Candy turned the engine, pumping the gas. At first, it stalled, but then it sputtered to life with a loud blast following a gray puff of smoke from the exhaust pipe. Candy rolled down the window and shouted at Valentine. "Thanks, man!"

Valentine closed the hood with a loud bang and wiped his hands on the back of his jeans. "No problem," he nodded.

He then turned his eyes on me. "You feeling better?" His eyes swept over my face, approvingly.

"Yep, I'm fine." I wiggled in my feet, trying to think what to say next. "Hmm... thanks for fixing the car."

He scratched his jaw, gazing at me through his thick, sooty lashes. "The battery cable was loose. But I wouldn't kill the engine 'til you get home."

127

"Yeah, good idea." I agreed as I handed the flash-light back. "Uh... thanks for catching me." It seemed weird admitting that I'd fainted.

"Any time." An awkward silence fell between us.

I glanced in the distance at a small flicker of light. A candle still burned in one of the windows, and then I asked, "Do you believe in magick?"

He sighed, smiling to himself. "I do. Among a few other things."

"I don't understand what is happening to me." His eyes held mine, quickening my pulse. "Maybe you could help me understand."

"I'd like that very much," Valentine whispered softly.

I was grateful the night hid my heated cheeks.

"I'm not sure you'll believe me."

Though I felt awkward, something in his man-ner soothed me. "I know. I haven't been very nice." I sighed. "I'm ready to listen."

He edged closer to me as I froze, unsure what to do. "Lots of eerie things go unnoticed in the bump of the night." His fingers slid sensuously over my bare arm, and a delicious shudder coursed through me. "I think once you open your mind to the wonders of the universe, you can begin to fully live."

"The universe is awfully vast."

"Do you wonder why you fainted?"

"I was dizzy," I whispered.

"You didn't just faint." Valentine fingered a strand of my hair.

"What do you mean?" I tried ignoring his closeness, but my heart thundered.

"Wendy never does anything without a solid reason. I think she senses you're special, Micki. That's why she invited you. Did you notice her two shadows were not by her side tonight?"

"Yeah, what's up with that?" I laughed, leaning against the car. "If that's true, she's mistaken. I'm not special."

"You don't see yourself like I do. You have a gift."

"I'm not the only one with a specialty," I flashed a shy smile. "Rescuing the damsel in distress seems to be a habit of yours."

Valentine chuckled. "It's not so bad." He leaned next to me, elbow propped on the hood. Our thighs touched.

"Uh… do you date?" His question just came from nowhere, and my heart suddenly lurched.

I shrugged. "Hmm… I guess. I've never been on a date."

Valentine edged a little closer. His breath cooled my cheeks. "I find that hard to believe."

"I've been asked a time or two. I never took anyone up on the offer."

"I'm assuming you've never been kissed either." His eyes danced with mirth.

I stiffened, momentarily abashed. "Hmm… nope."

"Well, beautiful, I hope I'm your first." Tenderly his eyes melted into mine. "Would you like to go to the Halloween Festival with me tomorrow night?"

Then my joy plummeted. "Uh, I promised Candy I'd go with him." Regret swallowed that pipe dream.

His brows pulled together. "Oh, I assumed Candy is gay. So, you are dating..."

"No." I shook my head. "Your assumption is correct. We're not dating. He's my best friend."

He cocked his head sideways as a swathe of curls fell over his eye. "Well, would you and Candy like to go with me to the festival?"

I bit my bottom lip, blocking a full-blown smile. "Let me talk to him, and I'll get back to you."

"No problem," Valentine grinned. "I'll see you at school tomorrow. You can tell me then."

"Okay. Thanks again for getting the car running." Awkwardness flushed my face.

"Don't mention it," he winked and then stepped away from the car. He nodded to Candy as he turned away, heading back.

As Candy and I drove off, I watched Valentine disappear back inside the barn. I exhaled a deep breath, feeling a swirl of mix emotions. What did he mean I had a gift. I never told anyone about seeing auras. I clenched my jaw. One more thing on my plate. Apart from his choice of friends, I liked Valentine more than I had anticipated. I saw the kindness in his eyes. And that *James Dean* vibe was working overtime. Nothing like a guy in a white T-shirt showing off his pecs and faded jeans hugging his swagger.

# Strife

Black clouds unfurled its wrath across the once star-filled night. Candy and I got about a mile down the road before a fierce gust of rain blew in, pounding everything in its path.

Candy swore that Wendy had put a curse on us. Our stupid car died and flooded several blocks from the house. We had to walk in the miserable down-pour. The icy rain bit through our skin as we fought to put one foot in front of the other. By the time we made it home, we both looked like drowned clowns with our black mascara running down our faces and saturated clothes hanging off our bodies.

After saying goodnight to Candy, I snuck into the house tiptoeing, hoping not to wake my dad. I was fooling myself. Louder than a herd of seals and con-taining more water than a tank, I clonked down the hall, leaving a trail of water.

When I passed the kitchen, Henry cleared his throat, startling me. In the dim light, he sat at the table with his fingers banded around his coffee mug. By the looks of the near-empty coffee pot and the grimace on his face, I gathered he'd been up for hours. I sensed my getting grounded was on the horizon.

"Young lady." His stern voice broke the quiet and stopped me dead in my tracks. My breath stalled as he went on to say, "You better have a good excuse. It's after one in the morning."

My pulse suddenly quickened when thunder roared, and a loud crackle of lightning flashed through the window. I swallowed the knot in my throat as I spoke. "Dad, I'm sorry. I'd forgotten my phone, and Candy didn't have his." I entered the kitchen and furthered my story. "Our car stalled, and we had to get this guy from school to fix it. We made it home all but five blocks. That's why I'm so wet." Water dripped off me, making a loud thumping off the wooden floor. "I really am sorry to have worried you. But I'm back and okay." I spotted my phone lying on the table next to Henry. I eased a breath of relief. At least he knew I wasn't lying.

"I see that. You have your own private swimming pool following you." Henry slid my phone across the table. "I suppose you didn't think to borrow someone's phone and call me. I would've come."

"I honestly didn't think to ask anyone. I was more worried about getting the car running." I eased out a breath. "I'm really sorry, Dad."

"All right. We'll talk about this tomorrow," Henry rose from the table, picking up his half-full cup and pouring the remaining in the sink and then flipping the switch to off on the coffee pot. "Be sure to charge your phone. I don't want you getting stuck somewhere in the middle of nowhere without a way to reach me."

"Yes, sir." I grabbed my phone and kissed Henry on the cheek. "Night, Dad."

"Goodnight, jellybean." The irritation in his tone had cooled, and my chest loosened. With my phone in my hand, I rushed upstairs.

After I finished toweling off, I dressed in my Santa Claus flannel pajamas that I'd gotten last Christmas from Joan. The material was soft to my skin and kept me snug and warm. I went down to the second floor to the linen closet and retrieved a second blanket. I couldn't shake this bone chill that rattled my teeth. I quickly spread the extra blanket on top of my thick feathered comforter and dove underneath. I buried my cold nose under the thick blankets and curled up into a ball. I considered turning the light off to stargaze as I fell asleep, but I was too cold to move.

Soon warmth began to spread its embracing wings, and I started to slip into a restful slumber. Deep in the crevice of my mind, candlelight flickered on the walls of my room, and the crackling of fire licked the back of my brain. A palm, smooth as silk, grazed my arm, ever so gently. The scent of sandalwood swirled between reality and fantasy. I inhaled deeply, drawing back a faint smile. My body shifted, moving down in the bed and closer to *him*. Lips, plump, and soft, lightly caressed my mouth. Taunting me as much as his delicious scent. He kissed the pulsing hollow at the base of my throat seductively as I felt a smooth palm coast under my top, pausing right below my breast as his mouth swooped down to capture mine. I eagerly surrendered, opening my mouth to receive his salty kisses. His tongue plunged deep, taking me with no mercy. Desire seized my mind as I rooted my fingers through his golden curls, pulling his lips to mine. His kisses were as skillful as he was *predatorial*. A faint whisper in my ears lingered. "You belong to me, beautiful."

Come six o'clock, my alarm went off. An annoying tune, *Who Let the Dogs Out*, pounded my foggy brain. I jolted upright as my eyes fluttered open. My dream flooded my mind as I blushed. In haste, I threw the covers off and raked in a frayed breath. My pajamas were still intact. "Man!" I whispered. "I don't recall ever having a dream as vivid as that one." Shivers gunned through me. Without thinking, I licked my swollen lips and tasted salt. Salt? When did I eat last? I hadn't been eating lately. I barely could hold down a Coke. And I loved my Coca-Cola. I shook off the dream and headed for the shower.

Dressed in my usual black, I rushed downstairs, taking two steps at a time. Henry was at the kitchen table, drinking another cup of coffee and reading the newspaper. Judging by the bags under his eyes, I'd bet my lunch money that he hadn't slept a wink. A sharp blow to my gut hit me. I blamed my self for that.

Henry's head snapped up. "Good-mornin' ta ya, Lassie!" he smiled big with his awful version of an

Irish accent. To hear him, one would never think he was from Ireland.

"Morning," I mumbled. I thought about trying cereal. Yet, I didn't want to get sick in front of my dad. He might insist I see a doctor. Whatever this was, a stomach virus, a cold, I wished it would run its course. Valentine came to mind, and I shoved the memory back down in the far back of my brain. I didn't care to deal with his tales from the crypt over breakfast.

I pulled a bowl down from the cabinet and grabbed a spoon and the box of corn flakes. After I prepared my breakfast, I joined Henry. I thought if I pushed the cereal around in my bowl, he wouldn't notice.

"Glad to see you're eating. I noticed you haven't been eating much. You're not trying to do some crazy diet, are you?" Henry peeked above the top of the newspaper, looking at me through his reading glasses, suspicion laid heavily in his eyes.

I squirmed in my chair. "No. Ew, Dad!" I dropped my gaze on the bowl and played with my spoon. "Hey, where's Grandpa?"

"He's sleeping in. You weren't the only one having a late night." Henry's face suddenly grew serious as he blew out a tiresome sigh, folding his newspaper and meeting my gaze. "I'm glad you made it home safely last night. The police found Susan Wallace's body in a field two miles from the Eastwick barn. The police aren't certain of the cause of death, but they found puncture wounds." Henry tossed the newspaper over into the trashcan behind him and gave a ragged sigh.

I dropped my spoon as milk splattered on the table. "You're kidding?" I gulped.

"I wish I were, jellybean." Henry's lips tightened into a straight line. "I don't want you going out to that barn anymore. You or Candy."

"No problem. I'll tell Candy."

He smiled, though it didn't match his tired eyes. It was a fact now. Knowing about the young girl, twisted my gut. The twelve-year-old kid was murdered. And the punctured wounds could only mean one thing... *vampires.* I knew Wendy and her fangers were behind this.

Henry cleared his throat and said, "I'm not grounding you for last night. I should. However, I have something to ask instead."

Oh geez! He was sending me back to Joan. My breath hinged in my throat, waiting for the blow. Henry cleared his voice and shifted in his seat. "I've met someone. A really nice lady too. We'd been dating secretly."

My chin almost hit the floor along with my stomach. "Why are you now telling me this?" That explained the late nights.

"I was going to tell you sooner, but then your issues with Phil, and you uprooted from your home and friends, I feared anything else would be too much."

"Dad, I wasn't exactly uprooted," I huffed. "First, I didn't have any friends to abandon. Leaving New

York was hard, but apart from that, I've preferred living with you. It was Mom's decision for me to live with her."

"I hate that you and your mother are at sorts. But I'm glad you're happy here, and there's no reason why you can't continue to stay with me after Grace and I marry."

"You're getting married?" I gawked. Did my ears deceive me?

Henry shook his head, staring down into his black coffee. "Listen, I'm not rushing into anything, but Grace is important to me, and I know the two of you will hit it off."

I remained quiet, unable to utter a word.

"I'd like to introduce you to her. Maybe this Sunday, we can invite her over for dinner?" Henry squeezed out a faint smile. The weariness in his blue eyes lodged a knot in my throat. I suspected he'd been missing sleep over this.

My left brow flew up, blankly staring at him like he'd shot me with a .44 mag pistol. "If you and this... *woman* decides to marry, will I live with you or boarding school?"

"Mick, *no!* This is your home too. You'll live here with us, of course."

"Us?" Good grief! He had the woman already moving in. Why couldn't he have done this when I'd left for college?

"How old is this woman?" I envisioned an old crippled crone wobbling on a cane.

"She's thirty-five. Same as me," Henry continued before I had the chance to respond. "Grace's family goes back centuries. The Eastwicks were the founders of this town. That barn you went to last night, it's a historical building. All her land has been in the family for centuries."

"So, most of her people are dead." My sarcasm reared its spiteful head.

"Let's try to be nice. Okay?" Henry shot me a firm gaze through his wire-rim, glasses.

I chewed the inside of my mouth, thinking. "All right. I promise to try." I changed the subject. "Oh, yeah, since I broke curfew last night, will you still be driving Candy and me to the festival tonight?" Needles pricked the back of my neck. I was certain the festival was off the table.

Henry cleared his throat. "I tell you what I'll do," he paused. "If you promise to meet Grace…and be on your best behavior, I'll let you go tonight, but you have a curfew, and you better stick to it this time. Home by eleven," his brow rose. "Deal?"

Internally, I spooled an eye roll. I knew a bribe when I heard one, but I could be bought. "Deal," I pushed my bowl to the side with my lips clamped into a pout.

Henry broke into a full smile. "Cool! It's settled. I'll take you then."

I wrinkled my nose. "Since we're bartering, I'll slap on an extra coat of sugar if you buy me a car." Low blow, but I had to give it a shot.

Henry snorted, "Nice try, kiddo. You don't even have a driver's license."

"I can take the test. I could apply for a hardship license."

"We'll talk about it later. Let's see how well you do with keeping curfew."

Ecstatic with hope, I broke into a broad smile. "Thanks, Dad." I leaped from my chair, realizing the time. "Oh, geez! I'm late. Gotta run!" I pecked Henry on the cheek and darted for the door, pausing to say, "See you tonight." I hurried out the door, sprinting across the lawn to the bus stop.

When we arrived at school, Candy and I fell in line with the other students exiting off the bus and heading inside through the usual doors. I took a detour to the girl's restroom, and Candy went to grab a book from his locker.

Down the hall and a sharp left, I pushed the restroom's door open when an iron-clad hand shoved me hard. I lost my balance and collided into the wall, smacking my forehead. "Ow!" I rubbed the forming bump. I turned about-face, meeting my assailant—*Wendy and her signature frown.* "What's your problem?" I glared at the fire-breathing dragon.

"To start with, you have a date with Valentine." Her voice stabbed at me like a sharp dagger. "Call it off. Now!"

"Wait! How did you know?" I gave her a sidelong glance of utter confusion.

"How do you think, stupid? I'm dating him."

Oh, geez! "I-I had no idea." I flung her hands off me. No way did I want to tie one on with this gal and her phony voodoo, but I had too much Hell's Kitchen in my blood to back down. "Valentine approached me."

"Why didn't you ask him if he had a girlfriend?"

My brows snapped together. "I didn't realize it was a requirement."

"Now you know. Valentine and I are an item."

"I think someone needs to tell your beau," I sneered.

"I advise you to steer clear of him. Unless you like sitting on lily pads eating flies."

I threw my hands up in surrender. "If Valentine's your boy, then why have you been letting him hang out with me?"

"Valentine has patience and can deal with it better than Diablo."

"What do you mean by "it"?" I demanded.

"It's when you change." Wendy's words smacked me in the forehead like a sledgehammer.

"You make this sound like you've done me a favor!" I stepped into her space. "You haven't. So, don't act like you're a good Samaritan. You hurt people, you callous witch!" I held my fists clenched to my side.

"Whatever!" She belted a chilly laugh.

"Who decided that I needed to be that creature's girlfriend anyway?" I looked her in the eye. "Was it you?"

"It doesn't matter now. It's too late. It's a matter of time before you cross. Accept and deal. And *FYI*... I don't make the calls." She shot a dark, cherry-red smile at me and spun on her heels out the restroom's door.

"Wait a minute! What do you mean cross?" I stayed on her heels. "I am so tired of everyone talking in riddles. Tell me!"

Wendy halted abruptly and faced me, her eyes hostile and calculating. "How should I know? I'm merely a broom-carrying witch. Ask Diablo."

"Have you been reading the newspaper lately?" I wanted to shake her up. "A girl from this school was found dead with puncture wounds. You know who murdered her, don't you?" I stepped up to Wendy, toe to toe, and lowered my voice. "I believe you and your little gang are to blame for her death and no telling how many others." There, I said it. I finally confronted her. It felt good too.

The irritation in Wendy's glint ignited into raw anger. "If you're smart, you'll keep your nose out of my business," she hissed through gritted teeth. "And stay away from Valentine." Without uttering another word, Wendy turned on her heel and strode down the hall with a springy bounce, disappearing around the corner.

"Whew!" I blew out, leaning back against the wall, thankful for its support. Wendy thought she was slick. Her innocent act didn't fool me for a minute. I suspected she was the mastermind behind Diablo attacking me. I didn't need my spidey senses to tell me that either. Guilt was written all over her face.

I kept to myself for the rest of the day. I wasn't in the mood for talking. And every brush at the shoulder, sent me reeling.

All day Candy watched me with suspicious eyes. He knew I was troubled, but he didn't ask. I didn't want to involve him. I feared he might go to the police. Reporting Wendy and her gang would be a deadly mistake.

At lunch, Candy and I sat at our usual table. I peered out the window in a daze at the dark, gloomy clouds that matched my mood. The scent of rain wafted in the air. Just our luck if a storm blew in, and Eastwick's Festival had to close. Whata bummer that would be.

"Why don't you come over and get ready at my house tonight. Bring your makeup." Candy drew me from my pity-party.

I arched a brow. "You plan to do my makeup?"

"Duh! Gul, I love ya, but you suck at applying that stuff." He bobbed his head and bugged his eyes out, acting silly.

I squinted at him, pretending to take offense. No point in denying it. "Okay, I suck at applying makeup. But give me paint and a brush, and I work miracles."

Minutes later, Candy and I were in a light conversation when Valentine approached our table. My eyes collided with his sultry eyes. "Hello! I assume you two made it home last night." Valentine's voice was smooth-edged and strong. He nodded at Candy and then focused his attention on me as a satisfying light

142

came into his eyes. I suddenly remembered my dream last night as my neck bristled.

Candy chimed in, "Yup, the car ran like a charm 'till we were five blocks from home. Sure glad it wasn't twenty."

Valentine belted out a musical laugh. "I hear you, my man." He then asked me in a gentle tone. "Can we talk?"

The tip of my ears heated from anger. "We can talk here if you don't mind. I don't want any repeats of your girl attacking me."

His expression clouded. "That's what I wanted to speak to you about."

Candy didn't say a word but sat there with his jaw dropped to the table. I nodded to Candy and said, "I'll be back." Then I cut my eyes back to Valentine. "Lead the way."

We stopped right outside the main entrance and perched on the steps. I hugged my waist, flinching every time the door burst open. I wasn't used to getting attacked by psychotic witches. Not fond of a repeat either.

I started off the conversation. I wasn't sure how to ask this, so I just spat it out. "Did you visit me in my bedroom last night?"

He arched a brow. "Why do you ask?"

"Just answer the question," I snapped.

"And if I did?"

My fingers fluttered to my neck. "If you wanted to kiss me, then you could've at least awakened me."

143

"I'll remember that." His violet eyes danced with mirth.

"What did you want to tell me?"

His face suddenly grew serious. "Wendy told me that she lost her temper with you. After an exchange of heated words, I warned her to stay away from you." His glint became soft as a caress. "I'm sorry this happened."

"Me too!" I scoffed. I was feeling the jealousy, and I refused to lie to myself any longer. I liked Valentine… *a lot*. Though, I was regretting it.

"Wendy lied. She's not my girlfriend, and we're not dating either."

"Then why would she come at me with her steel claws if the two of you haven't hooked up?"

Valentine hesitated, measuring me for a moment. "Micki, I never said Wendy and I hadn't been intimate. It's happened a couple of times. It meant nothing. The girl's free to be with any guy she wishes."

I scoffed. "You need to tell Wendy then. She believes you two are a couple." Not giving him time to respond, I went on to say, "and stay out of my bedroom." I shot him a furious glare and pivoted in my boots, leaving him where he plonked on the steps.

It looked like it was only Candy and me tonight. I shrugged off my disappointment and held my chin up. But deep down, my heart was breaking. No one told me about the woes of falling for a boy. First love was overrated.

# Evil Lurks

We decided that Henry had the duty to drop us off at the festival, and Ms. Mable had the privilege of picking us up.

That evening, I made my way to Candy's house. He promised to do my makeup. We were going all out with our costumes, though I wasn't sure how long the festival would last. I eyed the dark clouds. The weatherman stated an eighty percent chance of rain tonight. I hoped it held off until tomorrow.

When I knocked on the door, Candy's mother answered. "Come on in. How you are, chile? I'm Ms. Mable," she smiled broadly. Candy's mother stood not quite as tall though a little plumper than him. Like her son, she had a light tawny complexion with almond-shaped, green eyes. A beautiful woman, I'm guessing in her early forties.

"It's so nice to meet you, Ms. Mable," I smiled back.

"Gurrrl, look at your pretty self. You are beautiful. Candy said you were pretty, but he didn't say how gorgeous you were."

My face heated. "Thank you." I never liked it when someone pointed out my looks. I knew I was easy on the eyes. I'd even had offers to model. But I didn't want to be remembered as the pretty girl. I'd preferred to be thought of as an artist. "Is Candy in his room?"

"Yes, ma'am. You can go up. He's been talkin' all afternoon about doin' your makeup," Ms. Mable giggled softly.

"We've been planning this night for some time now," I hesitated. "Huh... you don't mind me going up to his room?" I was clueless if Candy's mom knew he was gay. I sure didn't plan to bring the subject up.

"Not at all. Go on up, honeychile." She patted my shoulder.

"Thanks, Ms. Mable," I smiled. "It was nice meeting you," I said as I darted upstairs.

Candy and I were going as drag queens. Of course, I was wearing my usual black but more feminine. A lacy top under a tight corset and leggings that revealed every curve of my body plus knee-high boots with spiked heels. Apart from my blonde hair, I looked a lot like the vampire slayer, Kate Beckinsale, in *Van Helsing. Candy curled my hair and painted my eyes a smoky gray.* I was amazed by the results. His talents were beyond this world. I didn't recognize myself in the mirror.

Candy wore an outfit similar to Van Helsing, the long trench coat and hat. Only he added loads of makeup. He reminded me of a young Prince. He had the best complexion too, like melted caramel. He stood tall and stunning, green eyes popping from his golden skin. I guaranteed heads would be turning tonight.

Rolling up to the entrance of the Eastwick fairgrounds, Henry dropped us off at the front gate and gave us both a list of what not to do and a long list of what to do if the situation rose to the occasion. Candy and I nodded and gave our respects, promising to behave.

Once we passed the booth with our tickets in hand, the exhilaration of the festival exploded between Candy and me. Laughter and screams permeated the park, and the aroma of corn dogs and funnel cake taunted our tummies. A good number of locals wearing Halloween costumes of bright orange and black, and then your typical fair share of witches and ghosts embellished the park. The festival covered a solid two-hundred acres with every inch decorated with jack-o-lanterns and neon orange lights strung from every corner, bathing the park in a soft tangerine glow.

Lots of games for spending coins, such as bobbing for apples, shooting yellow duckies, and then plenty of scary rides for the challenge.

As Candy and I headed for the Zipper, he straight up asked, "Why didn't you tell me about Wendy?"

I cringed internally.

147

"I didn't want you to go stomping off after her or Valentine."

"Still, you should've told me." The look on his face said it all... *hurt.*

"I didn't want you getting injured."

"I get what you're saying, but no mofo is gonna treat you that way as long as I'm around," his lips pursed.

I slipped my arm around his small waist and looked him straight in the eyes. "I'm sorry. Really."

"It's cool. But if you have a problem, tell me."

I smiled, misty-eyed. "I pinky swear." We locked each other's fingers together.

"Yo, pinky swear," his eyes gleamed. "Let's hit the rollercoaster." Candy grabbed my hand and took off in the opposite direction with me trying to keep in step in killer heels.

We screamed and laughed until our voices gave out. When the ride stopped, we staggered off and headed out. "Where to next?" I asked, still giggling.

"Let's check out the haunted house."

"Sounds great! Lead the way," I sang.

"I don't know if you know this, but Eastwick is infamous for its haunted houses," Candy boasted.

"Oh yeah? Nothing can beat New York's."

"I'll make a wager that we got y'all beat," he challenged.

When we reached the ride, we happily boarded the cart, and only moments later, we began to roll down the track. My heart pounded against my ribs, and Candy had a locked grip on my arm. I giggled at

148

his strained face. It warmed my heart to have my best buddy sharing the thrills. "Are you scared?" I asked, teasing.

"Gul, you know it!" He pressed his shoulder against mine.

"I'll protect you. You're safe with me." I squeezed his arm, flinching with a yap when a white ghost dropped in front of us. Candy nearly leaped in my lap, and I couldn't stop laughing.

When the ride ended, we headed for the food court. My throat burned so voraciously that I longed to suck a water-well dry.

Candy stepped up to the window while I sat at one of the tables under an awning. He ordered a funnel cake for himself and a large Coke for me.

We sat in silence as we listened to the sounds of the park. I greedily gulped down my drink, letting the cold liquid soothe my burning throat.

Between bites, Candy spoke. "I'm not one for mushy stuff, but I'm glad you moved here."

"Me too. I like living with my dad and Grandpa," I smiled. "I don't miss New York as much as I thought I would."

"My brother's absence had me hurtin' really bad, man. But since me and you've been hangin', I'm better. Can't wait for you to meet him." Then his face deepened with sorrow. "That is if he makes it back."

I reached over the table and squeezed his sticky hand. "Candy, don't say that. Your brother is coming back!" The swell of worry was apparent in his eyes.

"You hear me? He's coming back!" I said with conviction. Somehow, my spidey senses told me I was right.

He bounced one shoulder into a curt shrug, eyes down, picking at his cake. "Everyone good in my life leaves me."

"Boo, not everyone," my heart tugged. Candy's aura shifted into an orange, giving me an insight into how deep his pain went.

"Yeah, I hear you, but it still bugs me. First my dad and then my dog, Rerun, and now my brother." He looked at me, "We tight. If I lost you, I couldn't bear it."

I suddenly swallowed the knot in my throat. "Candy, no matter what, I am always your friend. I love you. You hear me? I'm here, and I'm not going anywhere. Okay?" I made him look at me. "I'm dead serious."

He shook his head and wiped a fallen tear from his cheek. "Sorry to get so cray-cray. I've never had a real friend before," he admitted shyly.

"Guess what? You're my first too. I've been mostly a loner myself," I smiled. "Boys like me but not enough to get to know me, and girls dislike me because the boys *chase* me," I paused. "And I'm not the friendliest person either."

Candy snorted. "You tellin' me!"

I laughed, air swatting him. "Shut up!"

When Candy finished his last bite of cake, we started to get up when unexpected visitors dropped down beside us. Pure alarm stabbed my chest as I didn't need an introduction. They were Valentine's blood brothers, the two bikers from the beach that night. What possible business did they have other than to cause trouble? The smell of evil clung to them, and I feared for my friend more than I feared for myself.

"Hello, ladies," Diablo spoke up, taking the liberties of throwing his musty arm around my shoulders and forcing me closer into the crevice of his armpit. I shot Candy a look of warning to stay quiet. "Where've you been hiding, gorgeous?" I leaned away, cringing from his touch. His stench reminded me of an alley over-flowing with rotten trash. New York had its moments in certain parts of the city, but this took center stage.

Wearing only a frayed vest, his pale chest glistened with a thin film of sweat in the faint light. I doubted Diablo ever bathed judging by the soil that clung to his skin and clothes—he was wearing the same leather vest, still covered in grime, from that night weeks ago. Tattooed from the neck down to his chest and arms, his body was swaddled in ink.

I noticed he bore the same tat as Valentine on his upper forearm. A Celtic knot, complete loops without any beginning or end, the mark of eternity. I wondered if it symbolized their gang, *The Sons of Blood*. I noted the other biker sitting next to Candy wore the same tat on his forearm as well.

"What do you want?" I asked with unwelcome frankness.

A wolfish smile etched into Diablo's face. "Why Micki, it hurts me that you find no pleasure in my company." He captured my gaze. "Let me officially introduce ourselves to your friend." I recalled that same Cajun voice. The same voice that invaded my nightmares. He placed his long-fingered hand on his chest. "I am Diablo, and this fine gentleman is Romeo." He pointed at his companion sitting next to Candy.

Romeo snapped a sharp salute without uttering a word.

"Please forgive my friend for his lack of patois. He lost his tongue in an unfortunate accident," Diablo explained.

"Leave us alone!" I attempted to break free of his iron grip, though his strength far surpassed mine.

"Is that how to treat your future mate?" Diablo chuckled, squeezing me tightly into his smelly armpit. I pushed down the bile that threatened to eject.

Romeo snaked his arm around Candy and held a long, razor-sharp fingernail to his throat like a dagger.

I gasped. "Don't hurt him!" I demanded through my gritted teeth. Aside from Romeo's unusually paled skin, he looked the part of a biker. Dirty russet hair past his shoulders, ratted in knots. His eyes, small and beady, darting this way and that, carefully surveying his surroundings like a predator. He also carried the same tattoo on his forearm as Diablo and Valentine.

Both men burst into laughter as Candy's face grew faint with panic. "Don't worry, pretty girl. We wish no harm to you or your little friend here." Diablo's sadistic laughter echoed into the crisp night air.

"What do you want?" I repeated with force.

He leaned his mouth to my ear and whispered, "You're becoming one of us. Embrace it, babee."

I jerked from Diablo's iron grip, but my efforts were futile. Powerless, I fired shards at Romeo as he held Candy dangerously close. "Let him go!" I choked out, fearing the worst. "I'll do anything you ask. Just let my friend go," I tried to appeal to their greed. It was the right thing to do. They were after me. Candy had nothing to do with this atrocity. He was innocent, and that was the problem. These beasts preyed on the weak.

Romeo looked me dead in the eye, drawing back a cluster of lascivious fangs. Taunting me, he took his sharp fingernail piercing Candy's neck. A thin stream of blood trailed down his throat and onto his white shirt. The biker drew back a smudge of blood on his finger and licked it. He then cut his eyes at me and flashed an unsavory grin.

Icy fear twisted my heart.

Unexpectedly, a peculiar urge seized me as my teeth grew razor sharp. I suddenly lusted for Candy's blood. My throat burned, aching for the dark crimson to quench the insatiable thirst that beseeched me. Shoving past the yearning, I gritted my teeth, demanding, "Get away from him and leave us!" My strange voice pierced my ears, so weird, so dark and deadly like a monster.

Candy's eyes orbed with horror. "Your eyes!"

My hand flew to my cheek as fright gusted over me.

Diablo whispered, "Whenever we hunger for blood, our eyes turn black, bruised veins puncture the skin, and we surrender to our primal instincts." He lifted his head from me and drew me into his trance, belting out this sick echoing laughter that twisted my stomach and enslaved my mind. I no longer could deny that I was becoming one of them. I stared at Candy's blood. The craving, the terrible craving that dominated my soul. I had to taste it. I never wanted anything as much as I ached to sink my teeth into his soft flesh.

Then Diablo pulled me back. "You will soon cross, my precious."

"No!" I hissed, tears streaming down my cheeks. I squeezed my eyes tight, fighting the dark thirst. I turned my head away. I couldn't look at Candy. The pleasant scent of his blood beckoned me. Its delicious aroma of sunflowers made my mouth water. The irrefutable craving seized my free will. I fought to resist, but I knew I couldn't hold on much longer. Reality shot through my mind. I was at a crossroad. Would I be strong enough to resist immortality or brave enough to confront death? The thought tore at my insides.

When I opened my eyes, I saw Candy, wide-eyed with shock and horror. Like punched in the gut, my past doubts had ceased. The horrific fate that Valentine had tried to warn me about, I finally unequivocally understood.

Diablo dragged my attention back by squeezing his long pointy fingers around my neck and whispering in my hair. His icy lips grazed my ear lobe, making me jolt from disgust. "Soon, you'll be mine."

Without warning, malevolent laughter squalled in the wind. Both men vanished in a blink, and in their place, a fetid flurry ripped through us, dust flying up into our eyes like a dirt devil on steroids. I hunkered down, covering my face with my sleeve.

When the thick cloud of dust settled, I opened my eyes and gaped at Candy's pallid face. I leaped from my seat and dashed to his side. "Oh, my God!" I choked out. "Candy, are you okay?" I grabbed a dozen napkins from the holder and started to gently dab his neck.

He abruptly snatched the napkins from my hand and snapped, "I'm fine! Keep your freaky self away from me. I ain't nobody's din-din." He covered his cut with the napkins, holding pressure to it. "Who were those two freaks? How the hell did they know you?"

I wiped my tears away with a napkin and began to explain. "Remember when I told you about getting attacked at the beach and how I thought they'd pranked me by forcing fake blood down my throat?" I paused. "The guy, Diablo, was my attacker. The quiet one, Romeo, was there too. He stayed back watching. Anyway, Valentine knocked Diablo off me, but not before he poured this disgusting thick sticky substance down my throat." My voice broke. "I-I think it was vampire blood. Valentine's been trying to help me, but I've been pushing him away and not listening to his warnings. I have no other choice but to admit that I'm changing into a blood-sucking monster.

That's why I've been sick. It all makes sense. I can't eat. My body is rejecting food. I see now that Valentine was right all along." I raked my fingers through my hair. "Valentine is like me. He's going through the change too. Soon he'll have to cross."

"What do you mean "cross"?" Candy's brows collided.

"It means the worst imaginable thing possible. Valentine and I will be forced to drink human blood." Getting out of this disaster was an impossibility. I was doomed, and I saw it in the reflection of Candy's terrified eyes.

"Why didn't you tell me this before now? This is the second time that you've kept me in the dark."

"I know. I was afraid, and I didn't believe it," I sniffled. "I'm so sorry."

"Let me get this straight." Candy responded sharply. "You mean to tell me that Valentine was there when that mofo, Diablo, attacked you? It sounds like your boy was part of the plan."

"I don't know." I averted my eyes, unable to face him.

"Yo, Valentine's weird. I saw that the first time I laid eyes on him."

"Maybe Wendy has some sorta spell over him. Why else would he hang out with her?"

Candy shook his head, twisting his face. "He's too invested to be innocent."

"Whether Valentine is or not, I need to stay away from him."

"I agree, gul."

"Something else. I think Diablo and Romeo killed that girl in our neighborhood. Her body was found not far from the barn." I swallowed the knot in my throat. "I think Wendy's involved somehow. I confronted her. She didn't confess, but I saw guilt in her eyes." I laid it all out there. Candy had three choices, either believe me or call me crazy. Or worse... *hate me forever.* After all, I almost sunk my fangs into him.

"Lord, have mercy!" Shock smothered his face. "You need to stay away from those psychos. And in the meantime, we need a magick potion to break this curse." His eyes drilled a hole to my soul or what was left of it.

"Wait! You believe me?" My brows knitted.

"Gul, this is Eastwick, Louisiana. The home of vampires and witches." He pressed the cut on his neck and flinched. "Those mofo creatures run amok here."

I sat there, my mind spinning. "If I didn't know any better, I'd think this was all a nightmare."

"That explains your strange behavior. How much blood did you drink?"

I shook my head. "I can't be certain. Maybe a couple of swallows." I sat there, stark-faced, horrified. "I'm going to lose everyone, my dad and Grandpa, and you," tears welled.

Candy reached over and took my hand. "We'll figure this out. Okay?" His voice calmed my panic. "C'mon. We need to get home, and until this cut heals, you keep your distance. I better not end up as your dinner or else I'm gonna be one mad dead person."

# Evil in the Breeze

When Ms. Mable drove up, Candy and I rushed to the car. We acted like everything was cool. Candy took the front seat, and I sat in the back.

It took no time before Ms. Mable spotted the gash on Candy's neck. "Mercy me! What in the world did you do to yourself?"

I didn't utter a word, though guilt racked my mind. This was my fault. Confessing felt like a huge relief, but I feared it would make matters worse, so I kept my mouth shut.

Candy insisted I not say a word. I doubted Ms. Mable would believe me anyway. Still, we decided the fewer people involved, the better. We made a pinky swear that neither parent would know.

"I ran into a sharp piece of metal. It ain't nothin'." Candy shrugged and then flinched.

"Son, it doesn't look like nothin' to me!" Ms. Mable's dark brow dipped into a V. "We goin' to the E.R. A doctor needs to have a look at you." Then

Ms. Mable tossed over her shoulder. "Chile, call your daddy, and let him know you're gonna be a little late."

"Yes, ma'am," Once we got to the hospital, I hung back outside to call Henry. I patted down my pockets for my phone and eased out a breath of relief. At least one thing was going right tonight.

The doctor examined Candy's laceration and wasted no time pulling out the supplies—surgical thread, gauze, antiseptic, a funny pair of scissors, and other supplies that I didn't recognize. Considering all the blood-loss, it was no surprise he needed stitches.

When Ms. Mable and I were waiting in the lobby, I soon discovered the consequences of lying to Candy's mama. Though Candy let the fib roll smoothly off his tongue like honey on a biscuit, his mom saw right through our farce. As a result, I got interrogated. I remembered her questions verbatim.

Ms. Mable cleared her throat as she laid her hands in her lap and pointed her gaze at me. "I may be from this swamp town, workin' on a waitress's salary, but I do know a lie when I hear one." She stared me at me as if gazing through a crystal ball. Then she blurted it out. "Are you kids in no good trouble?" Her motherly voice reminded me of my dad. Strong and determined.

My eyes widened as my mouth mocked an O. "No. Of course not," I answered. "Candy wasn't looking where he was going is all." But no matter how well I spun the lie, it deepened my shame. If Candy hadn't been with me, he wouldn't be getting stitches. Or if I hadn't sent Valentine on his merry way, we would've had protection.

"If this is an accident, then why are you apologizing?"

My eyes widened, like a mouse trapped in the corner by a tomcat. "I mean, I'm sorry he's hurt is all."

Ms. Mable paused; her green eyes fixed on me. "I'm aware of the scary souls that lurk in the shadows of this godless town," she confessed.

My spidey senses told me that Ms. Mable had no intention of letting this go, and her aura was a bright blue. A warrior. One who stood firm in opposition. "Uh… like what?" I squirmed in my seat.

"Do you know what a soothsayer is?"

"Uh… someone like a psychic?" I wrung my hands, feeling antsy.

"You're right. I see beyond the realm of the living." She tapped her temple. "You don't have to tell me, but I see you're in trouble. It's coming from your Chakra, a bright teal."

"You can see my aura?" Shock flew through me.

"I see a lotta things, babee. I think when we get home, I'm gonna give you a reading."

I wrinkled my nose. "I'm really okay, Ms. Mable." I didn't sound too convincing even to myself. But I decided to stick to mine and Candy's original plan. I played the dumb blonde.

"Chile, it's no secret how close you two are. I'm glad Candy found a friend. It's been hard on him since his brother's been gone and then the disappearing of his dad. So, I hope you don't get my boy

161

mixed up in foolery." A thin line appeared between Ms. Mable's brow as she pinned me with her green eyes.

"Of course not." I feigned a smile back as I sunk into my seat. I wanted to disappear, become invisible. If I told Ms. Mable about Valentine and his biker-gang, *The Sons of Blood*, she'd tell my dad. And then they'd get the police involved. What a fatal mistake that would be.

After experiencing Diablo's lack of care for human life, I feared his retaliation. As long as he ran amok, no one was safe. Stupid me. Unknowingly, I walked Candy right into the nest of cold-blooded killers. Then I recalled the missing girls. A newfound fear pierced my heart. I had no proof of how that girl died, but with the puncture wounds and drained of blood, it wasn't hard to figure it out. But one thing I was sure of that I couldn't allow the same fate to happen to Candy. Somehow, I had to stop Diablo and that whole gang, but the big question was, how? My heart pounded against my ribs. No one could help me now. Not even Superman.

Finally, Candy stepped out with a fresh white gauze covering the wound. He was a little loopy from the pain medicine the doctor gave him. "Here, Mom," he handed Ms. Mable the prescription the doctor wrote. "Man, my neck hurts." He palmed the blood-stained gauze taped to his neck and winced.

"Ah babee, let's go get your medicine and then home. I'll fix you some hot chocolate." Ms. Mable smiled into Candy's droopy face and slipped her arm around him. My heart suddenly tugged. Watching Ms. Mable coddled Candy made me think of Joan and how much I missed her.

We finally got home after we stopped at the pharmacy. The doctor prescribed Candy Tylenol 3. He dragged himself to the couch and stretched out, grabbing a floppy pillow, tucking it gently under his head.

Ms. Mable went to the kitchen and returned a few minutes later with two large piping hot mugs in her hands. "Come with me, chile," she said as she handed mine to me and then gave the other one to droopy-eyed Candy. One look at his tired face and I anticipated he'd fall into a dreamless slumber the second his head hit the pillow. It'd been a rough night.

I breathed in a deep whiff of the hot cocoa and drew back a soft groan. The dark, rich aroma delighted my tummy and warmed my woes. A perfect remedy for all ailments. I took a slow sip, letting it slide down my singeing throat, soothing the pain. I wished I knew how to shake off this sore throat. It continued to linger.

Ms. Mable led me down the hall and into a small room. She flipped the light on, and I instantly stalled. "What is this?" I asked as my eyes combed over the space. I noted a table and a gold platter with pieces that looked like old bones, milky with symbols carved into the surface. What a strange collection to have in one's possession.

"What you're eyeballing is called oracle bones. It is ancient divination but most effective. I'd like to give you a reading," Ms. Mable asked, but I perceived it more as an order than choice. "Take a seat at the table." She pointed to one of the chairs.

"Hmm... I've had my fortune read before. I'm good. I need to get home. Dad's probably worried," I rambled on like an idiot.

Ms. Mable's brows shot into an affronted frown. Her left hand flew to her hip as she wagged her index finger in my face. "Suit yourself, but there's a dark spirit hovering over you. I see it!" Her lips pressed tight. "Whether I give you a reading or not, you can't hide. Evil breezes in the air, babee."

My face dropped as I gave a failed attempt to smile. The weight of her words laid heavy on my heart. I asked, "What do you see?"

"I see a troubled girl who's over her head with deathwalkers." Ms. Mable leaned in and whispered, "Louisiana is renowned for its peculiarity. Deathwalkers run amok in this town." She stepped back, surveying my face.

"What are deathwalkers?" Alarm seized my lungs.

"Chile, don't you know nothin'?" she scolded. "Vampires. They are creatures of the night." Her words stung like stones thrown at my head.

I gulped, "Have you ever been in the presence of one?"

"My great-great-grandfather. A sire bit him. One that lives in this very town of Eastwick. I was five when I saw him. It was July 4th, a sultry summer night, the crickets hummed, and there was a faint breeze. My family and I were on the river, watching fireworks. That's when he appeared on the bank, watching us from afar. He was tall, dark, and mighty. I remember as if it were yesterday."

"Did he attack you?"

"No. He wasn't there to feed. He merely observed, perhaps to connect at a distance. I sensed he missed his family." She inhaled a sharp breath. "The next day, they found his body washed up on the bank, a stake driven through his heart." Ms. Mable's green eyes roamed over the small room and then drew in a sharp breath. "If you are in any kinda trouble with the deathwalkers, you can come to me." Then her eyes glossed over as if staring into another place and time. "You are blessed with a gift. That's why they seek you out."

I nodded, freaking out inwardly. A gift? Valentine said the same thing to me. Too much of a coward to ask any further, I diverted to another subject. "Uh… that's quite a spine-chilling story. Does Candy know about…"

Ms. Mable interrupted, "I've never told him. I'm afraid he'd never sleep a wink. You mustn't worry. I take precautions. I feed that boy garlic like it's goin' out of style," she giggled softly.

"Garlic works?" My eyes widened.

An impish grin, smooth as butter, framed her face. "It does if I cast a protection spell along with the recipe."

"Oh," was the only reply I could say. After a moment of awkwardness, I excused myself. "Well, our conversation has been very enthralling," I swallowed, "but I need to get home. Dad will be worried."

"Chile, I see the trouble in your face." Her deep green eyes took on a hunted look. My pulse kicked up a beat. "Watch yourself, chile," she warned.

"Uh... thanks for the advice." I swallowed the knot of fright. "I'm really sorry about Candy's... uh... *accident.*" I made myself smile and ducked out the front door. I could feel her eyes watching me. Ms. Mable didn't believe our tale. Lying might be a sin, but sometimes one had to make an exception.

# Deathwalkers and Mélange

I sprinted to my house and spotted our empty driveway. No sign of Henry's truck or Grandpa's El Camino. No lights in the house either, only a dim light burning in the left window by the front door.

Both men must be having another late night with their secret flings. I shook that gross thought right out of my brain. Ew!

Once inside the house, I bolted the door and trudged upstairs to my bedroom. I flipped the lamp on next to my bed and then went back to my bedroom door and closed it.

A cold draft penetrated my skin as I picked up my sweater off the accent chair and shrugged it on. I inhaled a deep breath and eased it out. So much worry knotted my stomach. So many unanswered questions. I didn't know where to start. I wrapped my arms around my waist, fighting off the chill. Why were these monsters targeting me? And now possibly coming for Candy. Neither one of us deserved this. And then Ms. Mable's story only confirmed what I already knew. Vampires existed! I had been in denial, but now I had to confront this baneful curse. How could I fight something so much stronger than me?

A quick bout of anger struck as if hurling the vase of flowers across the room and shattering it against the wall would soften my foul mood.

But then, I heard *his* musical voice pierce the darkness. I gasped, spinning on my heels. My eyes collided with two violet eyes staring back at me. I jolted with a sharp scream.

In a flash, Valentine ushered me into his embrace, covering my mouth with his palm. "Nice pitch," he whispered. His lips stretched into a smile pressed against my ear as his arm snaked around my waist, drawing me tighter. "I'm not here to harm you, sweetheart."

When I nodded in compliance, he dropped his hand and released me. I twirled on my heels, facing him, full of fire. "You've got to stop sneaking up on me like this!" I hissed, shoving his chest with all my might.

But I missed, tripping over my own footing, and falling through him like a transparent ghost. I crashed to the floor with a thud, landing on my derrière. As confusion pulverized my mind, I shot shards at him. "I fell through you. How is that possible?" I shouted, scooting on my bum across the floor, putting distance between us. For the first time, I feared Valentine.

"I'm not human. At least part of me is not." His face twisted, tormented much like a human's but a human he was far from.

"Am I becoming like you?" I flung my words at him. I held my eyes to his face as I gathered myself off the floor.

"Something like that but not entirely," he drawled with distinct mockery.

I stood tall, shoulders back, not backing away. "You have my attention now."

Valentine sauntered to the window and perched on the sill, gazing outside. At first, he silently looked out onto the street, as though he was a million miles away. Then he began to speak in a soft tone, barely above a whisper, slow and precise. "I didn't tell you the entire truth. The blood in the bottle didn't come from Diablo."

I dropped down on the edge of my bed in a blank stare. As my brain spun on its axis, I realized my life was one cluster-horror after another. "If not Diablo's blood, then whose?" I asked without breathing.

He turned to me; his eyes glistened with sorrow as if he'd given up on all hope of existence. "The blood belongs to our sire."

"Our sire?" I gasped.

"Yes. That night at the beach, it was a setup. Diablo was to feed you the blood. Wendy assisted."

"So, it's true. Wendy knew?"

"Yes," he answered.

I knuckled my fists to my side. All at once, I wanted to punch a wall. "Why me?"

"There are many reasons why we are chosen."

"I'm not sure I follow you."

"A sire is a pureblood, a true vampire in every sense. There are only two ways to become a pureblood. Either you are born one, or you drink directly from the sire while the blood is still warm and coursing through the vein."

"I don't understand. What does this have to do with me?" My brows drew together in confusion.

"You have to understand the histories first," he hesitated. "As I was saying… only a pure vampire, a sire, can change a human into a hybrid, a hybrid vampire known as a deathwalker. Diablo and Romeo are hybrid vampires, deathwalkers. They are blessed with immortality and must feed on blood to sustain life, but they cannot turn a human into a vampire. Apart from their inhuman strength, they are slaves to their sire."

"So, if I drink the sire's blood, does that make me a deathwalker?" Should I feel relief that I no longer had ties to that monster, Diablo, or had my problems become more harrowing than I once thought? My gut roiled with terror.

"No, not yet." Valentine eased from the windowsill and made his way to the bed, sitting down next to me.

"So, what am I, then?" Our eyes locked and lingered a moment. This time I was ready to listen.

"You're like me, a mélange. We are in transition, waiting for *the crossing*. Unlike a sire born a vampire or their hybrids, deathwalkers, we still are human-like and can walk in daylight. But once we drink human blood, that is when we forsake our human form and become a creature of the night, a deathwalker. Powerful and deadly. Although a sire is much more lethal. They are almighty and our God."

"Then, why drink the blood?" It sounded so simple in my head.

"If you don't drink, you die."

"I don't get it. You're still normal. Well, except for that fading like a ghost thing."

"I'm human-*like*," he arched a brow. "I'm on borrowed time. Soon I'll have to cross."

So many questions swirled in my head. "What about Diablo? Am I still promised to him?" I shivered over the thought of Diablo putting his hands on me.

A glazed look of despair began to spread over Valentine's angelic face. "Yes. That part is true."

"Do you wish the same?" I whispered. I didn't care what this stupid sire or Diablo planned for me. I didn't care about Wendy. Valentine was here with me. Just the two of us alone in my attic.

His finger tenderly traced the line of my cheekbone as a yearning in his beautiful eyes lulled me. "I try not to dwell on things that are impossible."

"What do you mean?"

"How can I dream of something that cannot happen? I have nothing to offer you."

My brows knitted, "I don't need anything."

"I'm a drifter. A loner at best."

"I don't care," my voice broke. "I like you."

171

He smiled, tucking a strand of my hair behind my ear. "I like you too."

I bit my bottom lip, breaking a smile. I wished we were two normal teenagers, and a kiss would be a simple kiss. But we weren't normal at all. I saw that more than ever now. "Do you wish to cross? To drink?"

"I don't wish to become a murderer," he whispered. "I'm not like my brothers, Diablo and Romeo. They have no humanity left in them. No concern for life. When we cross, our compassion dies with our human self, and we evolve into a senseless beast." Sadness clouded his eyes. "It's getting harder for me to resist. Once we give in to the dark thirst, there is no return."

Chills spiraled down my spine. "How long have you been...?"

"A mélange? Only a few months. I'm not much older than you. I'm eighteen. However, my story is different from yours." Sadness veiled his face. "Diablo stumbled upon me unconscious, lying in decaying food in a dumpster. I was near death when he found me. Homeless and beaten by two men who jumped me. They ambushed me to steal my cash, but when they discovered I was penniless, they turned their rage on me. Diablo knew I was near death, and he offered me immortality. I took from the bottle greedily. But soon, I regretted it. Learning that I must kill to sustain my life seemed to be too high of a price."

"How long do we have before we ... *die*?" Horror poured over me.

"You still have time, unlike me." Bitterness danced in his eyes.

"There has to be a way to stop this madness," I insisted.

Valentine scoffed, "Diablo once told me if we staked the sire before we crossed, we'd free ourselves of the curse. Return back to being human. But he claimed it was merely a rumor, a folklore tale. No one knows for certain."

I leaped to my feet. "I don't care. If there is a slight chance of gaining our lives back, we have to try!"

"It's not that easy. A sire is a hundred times stronger, faster. He'll smell you coming."

"But if we succeed, we'll be free," I argued.

Valentine sprung to his feet, towering over me. "This idea is insane, Micki. It's not smart to go against the sire. Diablo was ordered to take Romeo's tongue for simply questioning the sire's commands. It will be ten times worse if the sire discovers we're scheming to kill him!"

I hesitated, taking in Valentine's features. Under the faint light of the moon, his face glistened with such profound beauty that it stole my breath away. The intensity the gentle light revealed touched my heart and gave me more determination to fight. "The way I see it … I'm already dead. I won't drink blood. I'm not turning into a bloodsucker like Diablo and his pal Romeo!" I spoke with conviction, determined to stick to my impasse.

"This is far too dangerous. Not just for you but for everyone you love. *Your family*," Valentine reminded me.

"My family is in danger already. I don't have any other choice, and I refuse to take this lying down." I flinched, swallowing back my burning throat.

"Your throat hurts?" Valentine whispered as tenderness filled his voice.

"Yes," I answered as I cradled my throat.

"The desire increases every day. Your thirst will become unbearable. And the more you resist, the harder it will be to fight the urge."

"It sounds like you're giving up."

"There is no way out." Valentine cupped my chin tenderly in his cool hand. "Don't you get it?" An angry blaze flickered in his eyes.

I twisted from him. "I get that we have a chance to break this curse. I'm taking my life back," I bit out. "Are you with me or not?"

Valentine stared into my eyes, his mind churning. "All right!" he bit out. "We have to prepare. Diablo told me about sacred trees, dogwood. The wood is pure. We have to make stakes and purify them with holy water. You or I can't touch dogwood or the water. It will burn our skin like acid. We need a human's help."

"I can get Candy to help us." A light of hope fluttered through me. "Who is the sire?"

Valentine's face dropped. "That's a big question. I don't know."

"How can you not know?" I glared at him.

174

"Like you, I drank from the bottle. Diablo was alone that night in the alley. He brought me to meet Wendy."

"I can't stand her. It's her fault I'm in this mess!" I gritted my teeth.

"I'm grateful for her generosity. I've been a loner most of my life. Unlike you, when I was a toddler, I lost my parents. They were busted for drugs and got sent up the river for drug trafficking. I'd been bounced around foster homes my entire life."

I was moved by his admission. "It must've been difficult for you."

"At times, yes. Then it got easier. Wendy gave me a home." He averted his eyes.

"That was nice of Wendy, but ..." I grated. "Don't you see she's using you too?"

He shrugged, his eyes saddened. "It doesn't matter. I'm lost, regardless."

"Valentine, there's hope if we can kill the sire," I licked my lips feeling the excitement that we might have a way out of this nightmare. "Don't you see? It's Wendy! She's the sire."

"No. That's not possible." His eyes collided with mine. "Wendy walks during the day. Leave her be. She's human. I can smell her blood."

"I'm still not convinced." I shook my head. "My gut tells me somehow she's the sire!"

Valentine sighed with exasperation. "It's not Wendy."

"Where do you live?"

175

"I live in the Eastwick barn with Diablo and Romeo. There is a living space in the back."

"Wendy gave you a place to stay in the barn?"

"Yes, but..."

"Why else would she put you up in that barn if she wasn't the sire. She wanted you close to her."

He was quiet for a minute. "Maybe, but I doubt it."

"How can you stand living with those dirty animals?" My rage was shining through. I hated Valentine's loyalty to them.

"I ignore them mostly." A faint smile touched his eyes.

"Diablo and Romeo have been changed by the same sire?"

"Yes. Diablo is our leader. He speaks to the sire."

"If he knows the sire, then we'll follow him." A rush of hope stoked my excitement.

"It doesn't work that way, Micki," Valentine grimaced. "The sire speaks to him through telepathy. Diablo has never seen the sire. No one has."

I took in a deep breath and eased it out. "Then how do we track down our sire?"

"A sire generally stays anonymous. That's how they have existed for centuries. However, they stay close to their mélange and deathwalkers. That fact can be in our favor."

"Valentine! Open your eyes. I can't believe you don't see it. The sire has to be Wendy. She gave you and those two thugs a home. She's always lurking around you and your blood brothers. Who else could the sire possibly be?" I insisted.

He raked his fingers through his golden hair, and then he said in a low, composed voice. "You make a convincing argument." He blew out a stream of breath and scratched his day-old stubble. That five o'clock shade around his jawline was a good look on him.

"When do we start?" I smiled back, embracing the invigoration.

"Tomorrow night," he sighed. "Since we're cutting down trees, it's best to do it late at night."

"I can get my dad's truck and buzz-saw."

"That will help. Can your friend get his hands on some holy water?"

"I think so. I'll talk to Candy."

Unexpectedly, Valentine's face grew somber as he drew me into his consoling arms. "I'm sorry you got caught up in this strange world of mine. I tried to stop Diablo that night on the beach, but when he is hell-bent on doing something, it is near impossible to stop him. He's stronger than me because he's been feeding for twenty years. Romeo has been by Diablo's side almost from the beginning." He reached up and fingered a strand of my hair. "I wish things were different."

"Diablo and Romeo hurt people, and so does Wendy. How can you stand to be in the same room as them?"

A shadow of remorse glinted behind his eyes. "I have nowhere to go. At seventeen, I ran away from my last foster home. I'd been living on the streets for months. When Diablo found me in that alley, I found a sense of belonging for the first time in my life. I'm not blind to Diablo and Romeo's dark nature," his jaw twitched. "Every time I hear of some girl missing, I know my brothers are to blame. They have a voracious appetite, and nothing can stop them. I don't want to be *like* them. So, I fade into the background, waiting."

"Waiting for what?" My brows tugged together into worry.

"I have two options. Either I cross over, killing an innocent. Or I give myself up to death," he paused. "Both are equally appealing."

Tears came to my eyes. I didn't want to think about Valentine dying or losing him to bloodlust. "You can't think like that." I touched his cheeks, the skin cold beneath my fingertips. "I can't imagine my life without you. You're too important to me."

"You mean that?" His eyes searched mine.

"Yes," I whispered. "I care about you. My dad would let you stay here and give you a job."

Valentine chuckled. "Your dad would do that for me, a homeless boy that's interested in his daughter?"

"Yes," I giggled. "Dad's kind like that."

"Micki," he sighed. "I wish I could see through your eyes. The world would be so much better."

"We have to try," I whispered. "I can't become like your blood brothers, and I won't let you cross either." I paused. "I refuse to become a stupid newspaper headline, *Girl Lost*. But I'm feeling the change too." Reliving mine and Candy's encounter tonight sent shivers down my back. "Diablo and Romeo were at the festival tonight. They hurt Candy. When I saw Candy's blood, I'd never desired anything more. My teeth became jagged, sharp like blades." I held my breath. "I don't want to become a creature of the night, and I don't want to be Diablo's mate. I refuse."

"I won't let that happen. He doesn't deserve you," Valentine shifted in his feet. "You must be pretty happy with Candy?"

I detected a little jealousy. "I love Candy. But it's not the kind of love you think. As I explained before, I love him like a brother."

Valentine's eyes danced with mirth, and a delicious shudder heated my cheeks. "I remember, but I thought maybe your relationship had changed. I see you holding hands and wrapped in each other's arms. I assumed…"

"We're not dating. Candy is my best friend. Nothing will change that."

"Once you cross everything will change. The person you are now will no longer exist, and it will become too dangerous for Candy to be anywhere near you. Dangerous for any human."

Tears gathered, clouding my vision. "We have to fix this. I can't lose the people I love or worse, hurt them."

Valentine gently thumbed a fallen tear from my cheek as his eyes grew warm and gentle. "If I were a normal boy, I would've taken you on a date and stolen a kiss." He leaned closer to me, and my pulse quickened.

"But I'm not a normal girl." Our eyes locked. "Even when I was human," I whispered, unable to peel my eyes away.

Valentine swept me, weightless, into his arms as his mouth covered mine hungrily. I curled my fingers into his thick-golden curls and returned his kisses with openness. His hands began to explore the hollows of my back, drawing me closer, and I found myself wrapped in a cocoon of sweet desire.

I had to be honest with myself, I was falling for him, and though it thrilled me, it frightened me just as much.

When Valentine released my lips, he grazed his thumb across my moist cheek once more. "I'll handle Diablo and Romeo," he whispered tenderly. "They won't bother you or your friend anymore. And we will figure this nightmare out together. You have my word." He gathered me into his arms and held me snugly to his chest.

# Dinner Guest

"Candy, I know this sounds crazy, but I'm telling you that Wendy is the sire." I wholeheartedly believed this. "Valentine said that the sire never strays far from his vampires," I argued, standing in the middle of Candy's bedroom. Candy and I had the house to ourselves. Ms. Mable was working late.

"Is a sire female or male?"

"Uh, how should I know? Why?"

"Cuss you believe any old thang that mofo vampire says?" Candy pursed his lips.

"He's half. A half-vampire like me," I clarified, folding my arms across my chest.

"None of this makes no sense!" Candy shook his head as if knocking my idea out of his brain. "What difference does it make anyhow? Valentine's still gonna eat you!"

"No, he won't hurt me, and Valentine doesn't think Wendy is the sire. I do! This is my idea."

Candy's square jaw tightened as he tilted his chin, hands on his hips, full of attitude. "Listen, I'll be the first to say that Wendy is a witch. The only thang missin' is her wart. The broomstick is already up her butt. But that ho being the sire is really pushin' it, boo."

"Look, I gotta plan. We fill an empty bottle with holy water, and when you pass by Wendy, act like you tripped and pour the water on her. If she's a vampire, it will burn her. If it doesn't, then we have our answer. She's only a miserable witch. It's that simple." I shrugged, throwing my arms in the air. "Oh! We can throw in garlic too."

"Boo, garlic doesn't do nothin'. You watch too many vampire movies," Candy spat.

"I got that idea from your mom," I snorted.

"Keep my mama outta this! Besides, I don't hear *"we"* in this! Let's say Wendy is the sire, and you want me to walk my mofo butt up to a deadly vampire and throw burning water on her. Have you lost your dang mind?" Candy refused to see the reasoning behind my theory.

I dropped on his bed. "I can't touch holy water, or else I get burned," I begged. "I need your help. I can't do this alone."

"Okay, I'll do it, but don't expect to spend the night over her' no mo until we get this problem resolved. I don't wanna be no bloodsucker's dinner. Imma tart but not *that* kinda tart."

"Is that something like a sour grape?" I jabbed.

"Don't get snooty with me," Candy huffed. "Git home. You're on my last dang nerve."

I checked the time on my phone. "Crap! I'm late. Our dinner guest will be arriving any minute."

"Dinner guest? And you didn't invite me. Yo, I could eat." He stuck his lip out.

"Why don't you come. You'll be a distraction. It's my dad's new girlfriend. I think it's serious." My face soured like I'd eaten a truckload of lemons.

"Boo, I feel ya. I don't know what I'd do if Mama got a beau. I'd have to run him off. I ain't havin' no man up in my house."

"I know this is hard to hear, but your mom has a right to happiness. It's not like we're going to be living at home forever."

"Speak for yourself!" Candy's voice shot up. "I am perfectly happy living with my mama," he pursed his lips.

"Oh, brother! C'mon," I waved my hand. "Grab your English homework. We can do it together after dinner. I'll do anything to keep from having to chat with this woman."

"Dang! I thought I'd get to watch the fireworks between you and your daddy's girlfriend."

"Stop it! Or else you can stay home," I frowned. "Oh, by the way, Valentine is coming over tonight after Dad's asleep. You and I are going to help him gather dogwood and holy water. You said you'd help." I shot him a sly smile.

"Eh, my mama's got radar ears. She'll hear me sneaking out. No can do," Candy tossed a shrug.

"Then, spend the night with me. Dad sleeps like a dead log."

"Am I gonna be safe sleepin' 'round you?" Candy eyed me suspiciously.

I sputtered, laughing. "Of course."

With both of our arms loaded with Candy's homework and his art projects, we tore through the door and hustled upstairs.

Henry called out to me, "Can you wear something nice, please. Only you and me tonight. Grandpa has a date," he smiled. "Hurry! I'm expecting Grace any minute."

I yelled back down the stairs, "I will, and can you set an extra plate for Candy."

"Consider it done," Henry shouted back.

I closed my door and went to my stuffed closet. It was a mess. Half of my clothes were on the floor. I really needed to be more organized. I stared at my clutter. I spotted my favorite dress that was hanging on a wire hanger. I reached for it and began slipping off my shirt until I heard Candy screech. "Wait! Did you forget? I'm standin' 'ere." He held his hands over his eyes.

"Sorry, dude. I forgot."

"Don't dude me. I'm a dudette, okay?"

"Is that even a word?" I laughed.

"I'm gonna wait outside." Candy stomped to the door, shutting it with a loud thud.

I giggled, shaking my head. He never ceased to make me laugh. I slipped on my dress and then called out, "I'm decent now." I was sitting on my bed, tugging on my boots.

Candy creaked the door barely open and asked. "Are you sure? I don't need no mo scares."

I rolled my eyes. "Dudette, you've seen more on TV."

"It's different on TV. Wait a minute! How do you know what I watch?" Then he eyeballed my telescope sitting on its stand as his ears blistered. "Have you been peepin' at me in my drawers?"

"Ew! No." I laughed. "Well, once. Only for a second," I admitted.

Candy's mouth dropped open like he was catching flies. "I can't believe you'd do that."

"It was an accident. Trust me, I didn't look for long."

"Gul, you shouldn't be spyin' on no one. That's not right!"

"I don't spy. I gaze at stars. I only look at the neighbors when I see something interesting." I huffed with frustration. "C'mon. Let's go get this dinner over with. Remember, we have to call it a short night and do our homework. Midnight, Valentine is meeting us at the end of the block. I already put Henry's chainsaw in the back of his truck."

"You ain't teasin' me. We're really gonna chop down people's trees?"

"Yep, we are," I reassured him.

"I can't believe you volunteered me for this crazy muck."

I slapped Candy on the back. "What are friends for?"

Every year when the weather shifted to a crisp chill, and the trees began to drop leaves, Henry prepared his famous chili. The delightful aroma drifted through the house as we headed downstairs.

Just when the cornbread and salad were set on the table, the doorbell rang. I froze and shared a despairing glance with Candy. At this moment, I desperately wished I were Grandpa. He had a date. Gosh, I didn't want to meet this lady. If Henry needed to date this woman, fine! I wished he'd kept me in the dark. Or better, wait until I moved off to college. Then I wouldn't have to watch them smooch. Ew! I knew I was acting like a brat. Since Joan and Henry's divorce, I had to share at least one parent with a stranger. I always had Henry's full attention. But now even that was changing, and I wasn't pleased about it.

When Henry answered the door, I heard a soft musical voice enter the foyer. I stiffened, standing in the dining room next to Candy, keeping quiet and listening. He noticed my fidgeting and covered my hand with his own to ease my nerves. He smiled at me, and I returned a nervous smile back. It was time to put on fake happy faces, and I hated fake.

Henry sounded happy to see her. A brief silence drifted in the air as the sounds of lips smacking followed closely behind. Ew! I made a bitter face worse than if I'd eaten a bug. Candy nudged me and shook his head vehemently for me to keep silent. I rolled my eyes at him. I didn't think he got the full picture here.

This was my dad. The threat of a stranger taking him away ripped through my heart. I went through this with Joan and now my dad...

With his arm gently around the woman's shoulders, Henry and his lady entered the dining room. His face was bright, smiling as though he'd won the lottery. I wished. "Grace, I'd like for you to meet my daughter, Micki. We call her, Mick." Henry slid his arm over my shoulder and said, "Honey, this is Grace Eastwick." He smiled into her porcelain face.

I was stunned for a moment over her beauty. Thirty-something, about five-eight in height, fair skin, and delicate features, she reminded me of a Japanese geisha. Long cascading black hair and deep penetrating eyes, like the gemstone, Onyx.

She extended her delicate hand. "It is a pleasure meeting you. May I call you Mick?" She flashed her too white, too straight teeth.

"It's Micki," I announced firmly. I wasn't sold on her yet. The woman was a quick read. She came from money. Toting a Fendi bag and shoes and a killer dress to match was a dead giveaway. Too much perfume, though. I coughed when she stepped into my personal space.

Candy loudly cleared his throat as if he'd swallowed a fishbone. I cut my eyes at him with a grave look of warning. I knew I was less than gracious. But I couldn't help myself. I disliked this woman. There was no reasoning behind it, other than my radar detector was tripping out.

Henry interrupted, "Shall we have a seat at the table?" He gestured to the chairs. "Grace, please sit to my left and Mick, come sit on my right. Oh, yes, I'm terribly sorry." Henry pointed to Candy. "This is our neighbor and Mick's best friend, Elwood."

"So, pleased to meet you, Elwood." She flashed a generous smile and extended her hand.

"Likewise, ma'am." Candy busted into a broad smile and seemed to have lost his footing as he stumbled to take his seat. I didn't hesitate to kick him under the table. "Ouch!" he mumbled, glaring at me as I matched his. Candy didn't need to be so polite and make goo-goo eyes at the woman. He didn't even like girls!

Henry was showing his domestic side tonight. After he filled everyone's bowl, he sat at the head of the table, and that was when everything went south. "Tell me, dear, what do you think of our little town, Eastwick?" she asked in a cavalier tone.

I slurped my chili and swallowed before I answered. "It's fine." I didn't elaborate.

A sardonic smile grew across her face. "I should introduce you to my daughter. The two of you can go shopping. She has fabulous taste in clothes. Perhaps she could give you a few pointers."

I held Miss Eastwick's gaze and flashed her a sugarcane smile. "That's quite nice of you. Maybe I could teach your daughter how to jump through flaming hoops." Okay, I was a bit catty.

Henry's eyes darted straight at me, and Grace flashed a counterfeit smile as she sang. "Perhaps you know my daughter from school. The two of you are about the same age. Wendy?"

I suddenly strangled on my tea, coughing into my napkin. "Uh, I know a Wendy Belle."

"Yes, that's my daughter."

"I thought your name is Eastwick?" I stared at her, wondering how unlucky I could be?

"Yes. That is correct. Since my husband's death, I went back to using my maiden name. It's easier. All my businesses are in my family's last name, Eastwick."

Henry cleared his throat and interjected, "Grace is my business partner. She's an expert when it comes to the housing market. I owe my success to her."

I noticed that Candy kept his head down, spooning the chili in his mouth faster than he could swallow.

Pure alarm penetrated my skull. "You two are business partners?" Both Henry and Grace shared a sideways glance, and I nearly fell out of my chair. I gawked at Henry and then cut my glower at Grace. "Are you two planning to get married?" My mouth dropped open. "That's what this whole dinner is about. The two of you are engaged!" I looked at Henry like he was a stranger. "How long? Dad, I thought you said you've only known her a short while." I stared at him in utter disbelief.

Henry released a long sigh. "Honey, I've wanted to tell you, but I was waiting for the right time." A thin line deepened between his dark brows.

"Dad, this is a mistake. You barely know this woman!"

189

"Jellybean, I think in time, you will grow to love Grace." Henry patted me on the shoulder, smiling. I knew he was trying to console me, but my internal alarm system was screaming in my head. Something was off about her. I couldn't quite put my finger on it, but I felt it deep down to my bones.

Grace placed her well-manicured hand on Henry's arm and said, "Darling, I knew we should've waited. Maybe I should leave?" She laid her napkin down elegantly beside her bowl and started to gather to her feet, but Henry halted her by placing his hand over her delicate wrist.

"No. Mick needs to understand how important you are to me." Henry's words felt like a slap to the face.

I found myself speechless.

Almost.

"Yes, Dad, tell me, why don't you," I snapped.

Grace sat quietly with her hands folded in her lap as Henry's expression tightened. He answered, trying to hold back from yelling at me. "Honey, I know it's been tough for you since the divorce," he swallowed, pausing. "I didn't want to add more stress than you already have. Grace and I have been seeing each other for only a few weeks. The length of time doesn't matter. We are in love."

"Dad, I can't stop you from marrying this stranger. You've already made your mind up. But can you at least hold off the marriage until I go to college? I don't mean to sound selfish, but after dealing with a stepfather from hell, I'm not too keen on the idea of having a stepmother with the same bad behavior.

I can't deal." I didn't hold back my animosity against this female troll staring at me across the table. I instantly disliked her.

"Micki Lea O'Sullivan! That is enough. I understand you are upset, but I won't have you insult Grace."

"That's great! You sound like Mom, Dad."

"That's unfair. You haven't even given Grace a chance," Henry pointed out, but he halted on his next words when she placed her long fingers over his arm. He glanced at her with eyes of remorse. Embarrassment for his spoiled unreasonable daughter, I assumed.

I glanced at Candy. I noticed he'd finished his bowl and was eating his second piece of cornbread. Apart from him chomping his teeth, he wasn't making a sound. I slid my eyes back at Grace and then at Henry. "I've lost my appetite. I'm sorry." I threw my napkin on the table and leaped to my feet. I snatched Candy's arm and took flight out the front door, slamming it behind him.

As my mind whirled with madness, I trekked across the lawn, heading toward the end of the block. Candy's long legs stayed in step with mine. He called out to me. "Hold up! You can't walk out on Mr. B."

I stopped abruptly and fired my angry gaze at Candy. "I just did."

"You blowing up isn't gonna help the situation any. Kill da woman with kindness. Find out her weakness and use it against her."

191

A tumble of confused thoughts and feelings fluttered through my mind. "I normally don't act this way." I rooted my fingers through my hair as I realized more than ever how much my life was spiraling out of control.

Candy put his hand on my shoulder, his voice gentle and sincere. "I get you not liking this woman. I sensed something strange about her too. But it seems like your Dad is really crazy about her. He seems... *happy*."

"That's what makes it so hard." I spun on the heel of my boots and headed back to my house. "I gotta apologize." I looked over my shoulder at Candy as he stayed on my heels. "If I go full-blown bloodsucker, I'm gonna have to disappear. Dad is going to need someone to help him. It will tear him to pieces if he loses me. I saw what it did to him when he lost Mom. I have to set aside my selfishness and think about him." I halted at the door, my palm resting on the cool, metal knob.

"Don't make a big scene. Say your piece and exit to your bedroom. Don't engage in a conversation with the woman. Focus on your dad's face."

I nodded my head, agreeing. Taking a deep breath and running the words through my mind of what to say, I opened the door and stepped inside. I stopped in my tracks as my eyes fell on Dad and Grace lip-locked. Ew! Not exactly what I cared to see. I swallowed, lowering my gaze, and clearing my throat. Startled, Henry and Grace pulled from each other's embrace. Grace sported a smug smile. I kept my eyes averted from hers and addressed Henry only. "Dad," I continued. "Sorry for my outburst and walking out." I held my eyes to my boots and shifted in my feet. Guilt pummeled my mind for embarrassing Henry. But for Grace, my tank was empty of remorse.

Henry took a step toward me, but I held my hand out. "Please give me time to digest this. I really do want you happy, Dad." With that being said, I darted upstairs to my room with Candy, shyly shrugging at my dad and then trailing after me.

I leaned against the door, wrapping my arms around my waist. "That went better than I expected."

"Your dad has a ton of patience. My mama would've whooped my bee-hind with you still in the room. She don't play."

I think Candy idolized Henry. He was kind-hearted. Sometimes too kind.

"Yeah, a little too easy if you ask me." I suddenly got a wild idea and rushed to my yellow chair in the corner near the door. Quietly, I pulled the chair from the wall. These old Victorian homes carried noise through the vents. It was almost as good as an intercom. Dropping to my knees on the wooden floor, I held my ear to the vent. I looked at Candy and held my finger to my lips for him to be silent. He followed my lead and sat on the opposite side as we listened.

*"Darling, give her time. She'll come around. Micki is already easing into the idea of us together. Once we're married, we'll be one happy family. My Wendy and*

*your Micki will be sisters in every way. I will make sure of it."*

*"Grace,"* Henry's voice seemed careworn. *"Micki has been through hell and back with her mother and step-father. I don't want to upset her any more than she has been already."* I heard Henry blow out a weary sigh. *"I told you this was a mistake. She's not ready for me to move on with dating, much less a new wife."*

*"Then she needs to get used to it!"* Grace chided him.

I got the impression that Grace was losing grace. Her voice was sharp as a blade.

*"We don't have to move so fast,"* Henry suggested. *"We've only been seeing each other for six weeks. There's a lot that you and I need to know about each other before we can take our relationship to the next level."*

*"Darling, we are two adults. We both know we love each other, right?"* Grace's voice quickly softened, sirenic, and soothing.

*"Yes, of course, I love you. It's ... "* Henry broke off.

*"I understand completely. But children are resilient. I will make sure she and I become best friends. And she'll have a sister. Won't our family be blessed at holiday dinners?"*

Grace presented a compelling argument. I wasn't buying it. Silence drifted up through the vent and then the sound of a kiss. Ew! I pretended to stick my finger down my throat. Candy was holding his hand

194

over his mouth, cheeks puffy as if he was about to barf.

Then I heard Henry.

*"I think we should hold off family dinners for a bit until Micki is more comfortable with the idea of us as a couple. In a few months, she'll be attending college, and then maybe we can ease her into the idea of us getting married."*

*"Henry, I am not a patient woman for foolishness. Your daughter is acting like a spoiled brat!"* she hissed. *"Wendy would never behave with such disrespect as Micki has tonight."*

*"Grace, you don't understand what Micki has gone through."*

Quiet settled between them, and then it got bizarre.

*"Darling, look into my eyes,"* she paused. *"You will tell Micki that we are getting married in two weeks. Do you understand?"* Grace lulled.

*"Yes, my darling, I do."* Henry's voice appeared stiff and robotic.

Then the conversation ended as I heard footfalls and the front door open. They lingered a moment in the foyer. I could imagine what they were doing, and I instantly wanted to hurl. Then it dawned on me that if we heard them, they could hear us too.

I jumped to my feet and rushed, grabbing my tape from my desk drawer, and snatching the trash bag

195

that laid beside the wastebasket. I'd been planning to change bags but never got around to it. Good thing.

Back at the vent, I quickly taped the bag over the opening, making sure it was tight. I had gotten a nagging feeling that if Grace found out that we'd been eavesdropping on her conversation with Henry, there'd be hell to pay. This whole idea of marriage felt feigned. Even Henry didn't seem like himself. As if he was under an enchantment, he went along with whatever she asked. Nothing added up.

Candy jumped up to help me quietly push the chair back in its corner. Then I motioned for him to follow me to the other side of my room. The attic had plenty of room, like its own flat. Still, I worried our whispers might carry. I opened the window to the roof and waved for him to follow. "I think we're outta earshot out here," I spoke low. Candy and I took a seat on the slanted shingles. "Did you hear how strange my father sounded?" I chewed my nail.

"Which time?" Candy asked, staring at me with a blank face.

"*Dad*'s voice sounded strange as if hypnotized," I bit out through my teeth.

"I didn't hear that part. I heard Mr. B. saying he would rather wait."

I gaped at Candy, wondering if I heard Grace correctly. "They're getting married in two weeks. That disgusting woman was calling the shots." I ran my fingers through my hair and then buried my face in my palms.

Candy craned his neck. "Get down!" Panic soared through his whisper. "She's leaving."

I ducked down beside Candy and listened to the sounds of heels clicking across the pavement. In the next minute, I heard a car door shut, and the purr of an engine started. Then a bright, canary-yellow Porsche darted off.

"Grace proves the fact that not all rich people have good taste." I listened to the hum of the wheels fading down the street. When Grace's car was out of sight, we sat up, staring off down the quiet street.

"Yo, I'll take any Porsche," Candy's eyes gleamed. "Won't hear me complain." He craned his neck to see if he could catch another glimpse. I reacted by slapping the back of his noggin. "OW!" he ducked. "What the hell did you do that for?" He rubbed the crown of his head, shooting daggers at me.

"Don't go getting greedy on me. Remember, you're on my side," I reminded him.

"I ain't forgot. I'm merely admiring the car. Yonno, hate the driver, love the hot sports."

I rolled my eyes, "Whatever."

We peeled ourselves off the roof and climbed back inside, and Candy immediately started questioning the details about tonight. "Why does it have to be dogwood?" he shook his head. "I mean... we gotta bunch of trees in our backyard that needs thinning."

I walked over to my full-length mirror to straighten my hair. I turned to Candy and said, "I think it has to do with the tree having some kind of purity. Valentine didn't really go into too much detail." I flipped back around to the mirror and froze. My words jammed in my throat. "C-Candy! C'mere," I gaped at a faint line of my image. My body was barely visible.

Candy jumped to my side and froze, his skin paled. He kept opening his mouth and shutting it as if he were stumbling over what to say. He waved his hand in front of the mirror. Unlike my body, his hand was vivid. It looked like he'd stuck his hand through a ghost. "What the mofo?" he choked out.

I staggered back. Shock twined around my spine. My knees lost balance, and I tumbled to the floor with a loud thud.

Candy came to my side and helped me to my feet. Shaky and knocked silly, I could hardly stand without my knees buckling. He threw his arm around my waist and helped me to bed. I lifted my startled eyes at him. "What the hell? I'm fading into non-existence!"

Candy sat down beside me and threw his arm over my shoulders. "You ain't goin' nowhere. I got you, gul. You hear me? I got you!" His words were consoling like soothing balm over a cut. Racked with tears, I gave him a faint smile.

"You have to promise me something." I looked him in the eye. I knew he wasn't going to like this. "If our plan doesn't work, you have to stake me. I can't bear the notion of hurting you or my family," I choked out past my sobs.

The look in Candy's eyes said it all. Fear and determination. "You listen to me!" he grabbed my shoulder. "That ain't gonna happen to you. I won't let it. We're gonna stake Wendy before you cross. I am certain of that!"

I nodded my head, desperately wanting to believe him, but doubt seized my heart. I cried in his arms until my tears dried to nothing.

When I came to, I was stretched out on my bed, and Candy was sitting in the window sill staring off into the silver night. My eyes went straight for the mirror, and I spotted a throw-blanket draped over it. A smile came to me as I laid my head back onto my pillow and closed my eyes. I knew Candy couldn't protect me from the big, bad monster, though he knew how to make a bad situation feel not quite as bad. I loved him. Despite the risk, he stayed, looking out for me. But I couldn't let him get hurt or worse... *die.* I'd rather die a monster than live as one, and time was running out. This plan had to work or else...

# No Way Out

Midnight struck, and Henry was snoring loudly in his bed. I could hear him through the door. Without making a peep, Candy and I, with shoes in hand, tiptoed downstairs and out the back door heading for the garage at the side of the house. Before anyone was the wiser, I'd gathered all the tools we needed and swiped Henry's keys from the kitchen counter where he laid his junk every evening.

One last item I'd almost forgotten. *Gloves.* Henry kept thick work gloves hanging on a hook from his workstation in the garage. I pulled down two pairs off their hooks and whispered to Candy as I threw the gloves in the truck. "Hmm… we can't start the truck here because Dad will hear us." I pointed above us. "I'll put the truck in neutral and steer while you push."

"Hold on a dang minute! I didn't sign up for manual labor." Candy poked his lip out, pouting.

"Fine! You steer while I push. How hard can it be? The drive's all downhill." I placed my hands on the hood, arched my brow at Candy waiting for him to slide his long legs into the driver's seat.

When the truck rolled into the street and stopped, Candy scooted over as I jumped in the driver's seat and cranked up the engine, then off we sped. I didn't flip the lights on until a block from the house.

As soon as we coiled the corner, I spotted Valentine standing with his hands in his jean pockets, waiting at the curb. The moonlight glimmered over him; his beauty seized my breath. Liking Valentine right now when my life was such a chaotic mess was wacko. But whenever I saw his face, this giddiness bubbled inside me like a kid getting her first pony.

I pulled up beside Valentine as I rolled down the window. "Where's your bike?"

Valentine leaned his elbows in the window and planted a kiss on my lips. When he drew back, a smile toyed at the corners of his mouth, making me blush. He nodded to Candy before he answered me. "It's hidden in the brush." He nodded over his shoulder. "No one will bother it. Scoot over, I'll drive."

"Okay," I smiled, sliding to the middle of the seat. Driving Henry's old 1986 Ford truck was a hassle. Apart from its fading gold, it rattled more than any vehicle should. "Do you know where we can find dogwood trees?"

"I know exactly where a few trees grow. There's an orchard on Eastwick land."

"But aren't you afraid of getting caught and evicted? You live in their barn."

"It's an abandoned barn that no one ever bothers with except a few witches when the moon is full. Like Wendy and her clan," he winked.

"Did you know that Wendy is an Eastwick?"

"Yeah, I know," Valentine admitted.

"My dad is engaged to her mother. My worst nightmare."

Valentine's brow arched. "No joke!" He appeared surprised. "I've never met the grand mistress of Eastwick. What's she like?"

Candy interjected, "Apart from her sweet sports car, she's a snotty old crone with money."

Valentine chuckled. "Good man, you tell it like it is."

"I sure do. I ain't got time to play." Candy attempted to shrug, but I jabbed him in the ribs and shot him a dirty look.

"She's actually beautiful. Well-preserved for her age. Too young to be Wendy's mother."

"If she's half as aggressive as her daughter, I think I'll pass on meeting her." Valentine's lips parted in a smile, revealing straight, white teeth.

"I wish I could say the same. I can't believe my dad is falling for her. She's artificial."

"Artificial? How?" Valentine appeared curious.

"For starters, my dad is a great catch, but he's not rich. He's in debt up to his neck. Grace Eastwick is a socialite. She comes from old money. My dad and Queen Grace have nothing in common?"

Candy cleared his throat but kept quiet.

Valentine knuckled his mouth to keep from laughing. "Isn't it obvious?" He pinned my eyes to him.

"Ew! I don't want to think about my parents doing the deed." I slugged Valentine's upper arm. He flinched, laughing, palm up, shielding his arm.

Soon we came to the old dirt road of Eastwick and made a sharp turn. Henry's old truck wasn't as smooth as Candy's cousin's car. We jiggled, bumping shoulders as we rolled down the dark, deserted road.

A sudden bout of chills spread over my body. If I had the gift of looking into my future, I would've never expected to end up here. I slid a quick glance at Valentine and then at Candy. Strangely, I found two people who were very different from each other, and yet, I held them close to my heart. Candy, the best friend ever. Valentine, the silent broody type, perhaps defiant, kindled with a sort of passionate beauty. I inhaled a deep breath. He was definitely growing on me.

I had to be careful, though. Regardless of how beautiful those pools of violet were, I knew the pitfalls of falling for a boy like Valentine. If our plan didn't work, how much longer could he resist the dark thirst?

And if I were honest with myself, I was endangering Candy's life. What if I snapped one day and couldn't stop? The festival came to mind. What if next time I lose control?

I glanced again at Candy. He was hanging on to the strap above his head. By the strain on his face, I could tell he was uptight about our plans, but because of me, he was willing to risk his life. A pain of guilt hit. I was selfish, bringing Candy into this atrocity of mine.

As for Valentine, I had to keep him in the dark about the curve in my plan. He thought we were hunting for the sire, but I was still convinced it was Wendy. I planned to spill holy water on her and find out if my hunch was right. If my theory was wrong, no harm was done. We would proceed with plan B. Whatever that might be. But if my suspicions were correct, I'd stake Wendy, and this nightmare would be over. An easy cakewalk.

We turned off the road and through the field passed the barn, farther down to what looked like the back of Eastwick's property.

Valentine came to a stop and cut the engine. The three of us sat for a moment, staring ahead. Candy and I both dropped our mouths open. There lay an orchard of dogwood still full of leaves. "Why would someone grow so much?" I couldn't peel my eyes away.

"Maybe some mofo's planning on killing a bunch of vampires," Candy murmured.

"It seems the lady of Eastwick might be on to something," Valentine added, his eyes glued to the orchard.

"Yeah, it appears that way." I stared at the endless row of trees.

Valentine brought us out of our trance as he opened the squeaky door and urged, "We need to be quick." He jumped out of the truck, and I slid out on his side. He squeezed my waist gently to help me down but stalled, leaving his hands on my hips. "You look lovely under the moonlight." His satin voice soothed me as his eyes lingered on my lips.

I froze, lost in his soulful eyes. "Thanks," I whispered softly.

"This is dangerous. If the sire discovers our plan, we are dead."

My stomach twisted, aware of the peril we'd encounter if our plan failed. "It's a risk, but what other choice do we have? Neither one of us wants to cross. And I can't leave my father alone. Even if he's getting married to that broomstick witch."

A lopsided grin stretched across Valentine's face. "I seriously doubt that Grace Eastwick is a witch."

I huffed a sarcastic snort. "Even if she were, the woman is the least of my worries. Once this vampire problem is resolved, I planned to get rid of Grace."

Valentine shook his head, chuckling. "I hope I'm never on your bad side." He leaned in, and his lips pressed against mine, then gently covered my mouth. I melted in his arms, wishing we had all night to enjoy each other's embrace, but we didn't. I sighed when he dropped his hands from my waist, leaving me flushed.

Valentine grabbed the saw with his gloved hands and made his way through the dark to the farthest line of trees. Soon the sounds of a loud buzz pierced the night air as he began cutting up the small trees.

Candy and I hurried along, carrying sharpened stakes to the bed of the truck. I'd shared the other pair of gloves with Candy. He'd complained about getting calluses on his delicate palms, so I caved.

After what seemed like hours, we managed to wrap it up before the sun hit the trees. Valentine moved fluidly. I'd never witnessed anyone moving as swiftly. He blew my mind.

Then it happened.

Valentine started to lay the buzz-saw in the back of the truck, but when he swung to lift it up, Candy was in the way, and it nicked his arm. A thin line of crimson dripped down Candy's arm. Valentine and I both froze in our steps. Valentine spun on his heels and grabbed my arm. My eyes snapped up, and I gasped. His face was marked with black veins protruding from underneath his skin. His teeth morphed into something like canine teeth, or a better word... *fangs.* He spoke in a deep snarling voice. "Get Candy out of here. Now!" he hissed under his breath. Without a word, I nodded my head in agreement and twirled on my feet, rushing Candy to the truck. Fearing for the safety of my friend, I trembled, praying that Valentine would control himself.

In less than a second, all our hard work vanished. I stared at the back of the truck, my mouth gaping. The full bed of stakes gone, along with Valentine. It just happened all so fast. Mixed feelings surged through me.

Then Candy shoved my arm. "Let's get outta her'!" His voice verged on hysteria. I snapped out of it and started to jump in the driver's seat when I noticed two large stakes on the ground. Valentine must've dropped them. I swept them up into my thick glove and quickly pitched them in the back of the truck.

In the next beat, we were hauling butt. The farther the distance, the safer we were. Once we reached the city limits, I turned to Candy and asked, "How's the cut looking?" The citrus scent of his blood drifted in the cab, but this time, it didn't bother me.

Candy palmed his arm, covering the injury and eyed me with caution. "I'm fine. It's only a scratch. But *damnnnnn!* Your boyfriend was gonna eat me," Candy screeched.

I shook my head. "That's not true. He stopped himself and removed himself from the temptation."

"Boo! I saw his face. That mofo made me almost piss in my pants."

"Okay. Now, that's TMI." I cringed, laughing, but inside, my heart pounded my chest. Valentine almost lost control, and Candy almost ended up dead. Geez!

"Take me home. I want the comforts of my house," Candy demanded.

"Hmm, we have one more stop to make." I bit my bottom lip waiting for him to flip out.

"Pray tell, what now?"

"The holy water." I looked at his puckered face.

A slew of curses rolled off Candy's tongue. "We gotta do that tonight?" Candy stuck his head out the window, and then he cut his eyes back at me. "How the hell are we gonna get into a church? It's after midnight."

"The cathedral on Bon Ton Street stays open for the homeless. They keep a tray of blessed water, twenty-four-seven." I tossed an empty milk jug across the seat. "Here. Fill this."

"Why can't you do it?" Candy shot green shards at me.

I held my arm out to show him the blisters where the dogwood had brushed my skin. "If a tree can do this to me, then what will holy water do? I really don't want to find out."

I rolled up to the curb and stopped directly in front of the church. It stood tall and impressive with its stained glass of many colors dating back to the nineteenth century.

"Fine! You owe me big time," Candy growled, hopping out of the truck as he stomped off toward the entrance of the church. I watched as he disappeared inside.

If I wasn't a believer before tonight, I certainly was wholly convinced now. Seeing Valentine's demonic face chilled my bones. If we didn't find the sire and kill it, Valentine and I were doomed.

Where was Superman when you needed him?

# Target

"You remember the plan, right?" I asked Candy as we headed through the doors at school.

"How can I forget? We rehearsed it a hundred times last night. You're lucky I'm standing up. I need my beauty sleep to function."

"There will be plenty of time to sleep after we stake Wendy," I whispered.

Candy's eyes bulged like frog eyes. "Hold on a mofo minute! I didn't agree to murder," he snarled under his breath.

"It's not murder if she's a vampire," I argued.

"So, you gonna stake her at lunch in front of the whole damn cafeteria?" He glowered at me like I'd been admitted to the crazy farm.

"No. We have to lure her to the park. No one is there during school hours. She goes there every day at third period. It's perfect."

"Not only are we gonna commit murder, but we're skippin' class too?"

I shrugged, rolling my eyes. "You got a better idea?"

"Yep! Forget this crazy notion, and I go home and fix me a piece of sweet potato pie." His hands flew to his hips and stuck his chin out, halting in the middle of the hallway.

I had to do some fast-talking. I licked my lips and said, "I get you're scared. Me too. I'm not going to do anything until I see if the holy water burns Wendy's skin. If Wendy's human, it won't affect her. Except maybe piss her off. And if that happens, we apologize and go home. No one dies."

"How do you know if the water is pure? The priest could've forgotten to bless it, and it's nothin' more than plain old water from the faucet."

I looked both ways down the hall and snatched up Candy's sleeve, dragging him around the corner where it was more private. "Give me the bottle." I held out my hand.

Candy's eyes widened. "What are you gonna do?"

"I plan to test the water. If it burns my skin, then we know it works."

"Are all white girls wacky as you?" He stared at me.

"I don't know. I haven't met all of them. But looking at the ratio, I'd say seventy to ninety percent of us white chicks are nuts."

"This ain't funny. What if it burns you to the bone? Then how will we explain that?"

"One drop can't do that much damage. Besides, I'll heal at once. Or I think I will."

"Gul, you still watchin' those vampire movies?"

"C'mon, we gotta get to class." I urged as I peered down the hall both ways.

Candy quickly pulled the bottle out of his book bag and twisted the cap off. "Only a drop," he confirmed.

I nodded, holding my palm out. Candy poured a drop in the cap and then slowly held it over my wrist. His emerald green eyes locked with mine, "You sure?"

"Yes. Just do it!"

Candy tilted the cap, only releasing a tiny drop onto the center of my wrist. When the water struck, steam curled and sizzled, setting my entire body into a spiral of raw agony. The foul stench of singeing skin penetrated my nose. "It works!" My tearful eyes locked with Candy's frightened face.

He quickly patted the remaining water off my wrist. "I'm so sorry to have even questioned you. This crap ain't nothin' to play with." His stark eyes held mine.

"Yeah, it's real." I flinched from the mind-blowing burn. Then after a few ticks passed, the wound disappeared, and so did the pain.

Candy and I both gaped at each other.

"It's gone!" Shock smothered his eyes.

Third period came, and Candy and I escaped past anyone's notice. Not wasting a minute, we headed for the park. There was a thick line of trees that encircled it. A perfect place to hide for the potheads and couples making out.

Once we cleared the brush, we spotted Wendy. To our advantage, she was alone. Candy and I shared a strained glance and proceeded with caution. I forced a smile on my face but then dropped it. I remembered that I never smiled at her. The last thing I wanted was to make her suspicious. Although I did have a solid reason to speak to her. Since our parents were engaged, I couldn't have had a more perfect excuse. *Thanks, Dad.*

Wendy's head snapped up in our direction as we came into sight. Of course, with Candy's big feet stepping on every branch on the ground, she could hear us a mile away. "How lovely of you to join me. Skipping class?" Wendy pitched her usual acidic smile that I'd grown to hate. She was sitting, knees crossed on top of the same picnic table from last time I visited the park, sucking on a cigarette.

"You and I need to talk." I held my shoulders straight, ready to go into action. "Do you know our parents are engaged?"

A smirk appeared across Wendy's face. "Yes. I hate the idea of having you for a sister too."

"Yeah, not my idea of a happy family, either."

"So, you want my help to break up the happy couple?" she snarled. "A little black magic, maybe?"

I glanced at Candy and then cut my eyes back at Wendy. "Sure. You got any clever ideas."

Wendy threw back her head and belted out laughter. "I have several."

"Let's chat." I slid a glance at Candy. Cue to get ready. I wrapped my fingers around one of the stakes inside my bag as my partner in crime trotted his way over by Wendy, pretending to take a seat. But when he started to make his fake trip, a deep voice pierced the air, and Candy stopped in his tracks.

"Students, don't you have class?"

I knew that voice from anywhere. Mrs. Jenkins, the principal, stood five-ten, packing a good two hundred pounds, pushing middle age, hair streaked with gray. Holding a steady scornful glare straight at us, hands clung to her hips. We were in big trouble. Just our luck too. Now I had to explain to my dad why I'd gotten expelled from school. Looked like it would be another week before we found out if Wendy was the sire.

Crap!

* * *

"Dad, I'm sorry. I know it was stupid." I might as well dig my grave now. Riding in the truck with an angry Henry was like walking a tightrope to my own execution. I didn't recall the last time I'd seen him this upset.

"Micki, I know you're going through some issues, but this is flat out defiance. What were you thinking, skipping class?" His shoulders were stiff, and his face tight and drawn. I hadn't noticed how gray Henry's brows were until now. He reminded me of a mad Santa Claus, only younger and thinner.

"I needed to talk to Wendy privately. I swear, Dad, as soon as I had finished, I was headed straight to class." I bit down on my bottom lip, staring out my window.

"That's no excuse. You could've approached your friend after school. Now you got Candy in trouble too. You're both suspended from school for three days, and I can't be certain if I can trust you to behave at home alone. Maybe Grandpa can watch you."

I blenched, hearing the anger in his tone. "I'm really sorry, Dad."

"I hope so, but you're grounded for three weeks. No friends coming over or going anywhere but school and home."

"Yes sir," I mumbled, feeling like a kicked dog. I was sure Candy was catching hell too from his mom. I felt even worse for him. It was apparent that being my sidekick was hazardous. I slipped a sideways glance at Henry. His face was void of his usual happiness. I sunk in my seat, feeling super guilty for my stupid idea.

"Look, I know you're not too happy with me getting engaged. But if you give Grace a chance, I think you will like her. And you've always wanted a sister."

Annoyance gnawed at my stomach. Henry had no idea the kind of person Wendy was. If my suspicions were right, there wouldn't be any issues. I planned to stake her in the chest and end her life. I was okay with that. "Dad, have you met Grace's demon child, Wendy?"

"Micki Lea O'Sullivan, that is not nice." Henry tightened his lips.

"You don't know Wendy like I do. She is the worst human being you will ever meet."

"Isn't that a bit extreme?" Henry shook his head.

But I kept my stance. "Nope. Not one bit."

"I have a feeling if you put on that sweet charm of yours, you and Wendy will be BFFs."

"Dad, I already have a BFF."

"There is always room for another," Henry countered.

I exhaled a depressed sigh. "I suppose." No point in arguing. Henry was dead set we were going to be one big happy family. He was in for a huge disappointment.

"Your mom called. She said she'd been trying to reach you all week. You should give her a buzz."

I rolled my eyes. "I've called Mom at least five times. She's now calling me."

"Give her a call. Talk out your issues with her. You'll feel better."

"How did that work for you?" I brought my knees to my chest and stared out my window.

"Your mother and I grew apart. There comes a point in time when you have to let things go. It's not worth holding on to the anger."

"I'll call her tonight," I shrugged.

Later that evening, Henry had given back my phone for the one purpose of calling Mom. I dreaded the talk too. I knew he'd ratted me out. Wasn't that what parents did? I tapped contacts and scrolled down to Joan's number. Moments later, I heard a "Hello."

"Hi, Mom. How's it going?" I sighed, full of dread.

"Hey there, honey! Sorry, I haven't called you back. I've been busy with this charity event for the homeless that I'm coordinating." Nervous silence wedged between us. "Hmm..., how do you like it there? I hope you're making friends."

"A couple," I answered with little enthusiasm.

"Listen, I know you're probably mad at me for sending you to your dad's. I thought... I thought it would be in your best interest. Phil was used to running a tight ship. He's not familiar with teenagers."

"Yeah, I know. He's a stiff suit." I knew my popping off hurt Joan, but I didn't understand why she took Phil's crap.

"Now that's not nice to say. Phil is paying for your college tuition, young lady."

I rolled my eyes. "Is that what he's been telling you?" I blew out an angry breath. "You should ask him if you can see his bank account."

"I'll do no such thing!" Joan snapped. "I trust Phil will come through when the time comes."

"Mom, why don't you leave him? He's kinder to his secretary. You know, the one with blonde hair and big boobs."

"Stop it, Micki! Why does it have to be a confrontation with you every time?" Her voice shook. I could only imagine Phil was getting worse.

"Has Phil hit you, Mom?" I straight up asked.

"He would never hit me," Joan denied. "Phil is a good man. He gets wound up is all. He's the owner of a prestigious law firm. Phil has a lot on his plate."

"That's no excuse to yell at you and talk down to you."

"Micki, your dad told me what happened at school. Why on heaven's earth would you skip class?" Now Joan was acting like a parent.

"Mom, it's one big misunderstanding. I intended to go to class." Lying was wrong but sometimes a necessary sin.

"Just promise me that you will stay out of trouble. I love you, but Phil is ready to send you to a reform school. So, don't make your dad send you back." I had no doubt what Phil would do.

"I promise I'll stay outta trouble. Okay?"

"Okay." Joan suddenly got quiet, and then she asked, "How is your dad?" She still loved Dad. I could hear it in her voice. I knew she regretted marrying Phil. And as history repeated itself, I suspected he was messing around with his new secretary. My spidey senses were hardly ever wrong.

"Dad has a fiancé."

Silence abraded over the phone. Then Joan cleared her throat. "Wow! I wasn't aware that he was dating."

"Me either, and I live with him." I dragged in a deep breath. "Dad said he's been dating her before I moved here. Apparently, he's been keeping her a secret."

"I guess so." Joan blasted a puff of air.

"Mom, it's late, and I have homework. I gotta go."

"Okay, honey. I'll talk to you soon." I sensed a faint smile from Joan's end.

"Yeah, soon." I hit the red button on my cell.

That night, I gazed through the skylight at the stars. They were brighter than usual tonight, I thought as my troubles churned in my brain. I sighed, feeling the brunt of my mistake today. So much burden to carry. I couldn't go to either parent. Letting Henry down killed me inside. I had to find my way out of this nightmare before I lose my family. I didn't want anyone else hurt. That included Candy. I wished I could call him. I went to my telescope by the window and pointed it at his bedroom. I leaned in and looked. I drew back with a long sigh. His light was out. What was the point in calling him? I suspected that Ms. Mable put an end to us hanging out anymore. It was for the best. If I'd lost control and hurt Candy, I would've never forgiven myself. The pain in my throat was intensifying. Seeing Valentine become a monster with my own eyes shook my world. His face distorted, his teeth protruding into sharp razors. The black veins that encased his eyes were insidious. An icy shiver skirted down the collar of my pajama top.

# The Sire

The past two days had become a blur. Since Henry had grounded me, I couldn't use my phone or watch television. I was going freaking crazy. I haven't been able to see Candy, and I suspect Henry and Ms. Mable had joined forces. My punishment felt more extreme than usual. Henry was a firm parent, but he usually softened. This time, he didn't budge an inch. I guess I really screwed up.

The three of us, Grandpa, Henry, and I, were sitting at the table while silence hovered over us. I picked at my peas and creamed potatoes. My appetite was declining faster than a mudslide. So far, I'd been sneaky enough to hide my lack of appetite. Slipping food in my pocket or anywhere he wouldn't find it became a daily chore for me.

I broke the silence. "Dad, I know I did wrong, but there's been something I've needed to ask you."

"You can talk to me about anything. What's troubling you?" he smiled.

I shifted in my seat, fearing he'd say, no. "Candy and his mom are having financial troubles."

"Yeah," he nodded.

"Well, I was wondering if you might have a position for her at work. You know, at the construction site. I imagine she'd be great at anything." I shrugged, trying not to push.

Henry scratched his day-old stubble, quiet for a moment. I assumed he was thinking about it. I crossed my fingers, holding my breath.

"Now that you mentioned it, I need someone to clean up the houses after we finish the site." He jabbed a bite of steak, chewed for a couple of seconds, then swallowed. "I'll talk to Ms. Mable after dinner," he smiled. "You're awfully nice to think about them."

I pressed a smile. "Thanks."

Grandpa spoke up. "Of course, she's nice. My granddaughter, even when she was a tiny lassie, thought of others before herself. Now house cleaning is another story." He bellowed, jiggling, pointing his fork at me.

"Grandpa!" I laughed, shoving my potatoes into a small mound.

I looked at Henry and said, "Thanks, Dad." My eyes filled with moisture. I did care. Candy was family to me. I couldn't bear seeing them go without food. At least when I was gone, I'd know that Candy's life would be better. I hope his brother comes back. Candy and Ms. Mable wouldn't be alone.

After dinner, I climbed the three flights of stairs to my bedroom. Since I was grounded from everything that was slightly entertaining, I decided to get out my art pencils. I'd been neglecting my craft. Henry had gone to the trouble of buying me a drafting table, and I had yet to use it. He installed a light over the table, illuminating a perfect setting. I pulled out all my paint supplies and pad. I started with my circles and formatting. I thought I'd go with the mood and see what I ended up sketching.

When I'd finished, I held the sketch up to examine the flaws and drew back a gasp. My eyes combed over a flawless ébauche of Valentine's face. His soft honey hair blowing in the gentle breeze. His eyes, intense, drilling a hole into my soul. I sighed.

It dawned on me how little I knew about this boy. Other than his childhood as an orphan, shuffled from one foster home to another, I knew nothing else. I wondered if he had any interests? Did he like vanilla ice cream? I laughed at myself, full of sarcasm... *no, he liked blood.*

I dropped my pad and moved from the table to flopping down on my bed. I bounced a couple of times before I settled into the soft white cushion of my bedding. My eyes washed over the large room. Its perimeter covered the same square footage as the second floor. When Henry first bought the house, the attic started out not much more than plank flooring and boarded walls, collecting junk and cobwebs. But then the transformation came. Since Henry's modifications when I first moved here, I decided to add more string-lights, multiple colors lining the vaulted ceiling. My painting skills came in handy. I painted murals on the walls of colorful flowers and cute girls with round rosy cheeks and oversized eyes. And poems. Some I had written, and others came from childhood. I loved the one in the book, Dean's, Mother Goose. *Millions of Massive Raindrops*. When my parents were still together, I remembered Henry and Joan would tuck me in reading this poem. I'd have them read it over and over until I drifted off to sleep. I drew in a long breath as my eyes carefully washed over my art. I liked to think of my walls as a collection of me, the past, the present, and the future. Or at least two out of three. I wasn't so sure about my future.

* * *

I was awakened by a faint stir. My eyes fluttered opened as I caught a glance of the moon. Its light filtered through the window, bathing my room in a soft silvery glow. I lay there, staring out and listening to the gentle brush of the trees swaying to the breeze. Henry must be asleep. I didn't hear the gentle hum of the television. I eased out a breath and caught a scent. A woodsy scent.

*Valentine!*

I jolted to a sitting position as my eyes brushed over my room. I gasped when my gaze landed on a silhouette standing back in the shadows. I kicked off the covers and bolted to my feet. "How do you keep sneaking in my room?" I bit out. "Seriously! You have to stop creeping up on me." I flexed my fists to my side, ready to sock him, but then I remembered the last time I tried that.

He slowly stepped out. "Hmm... nice drawing," he tilted his chiseled chin toward my pad on the draft table as a faint smile teased his lips.

A rush of embarrassment swept over me. I didn't intend for anyone to see my work. "Really Valentine, you've got to stop creeping up on me like this. Some things are meant to be private." I stomped over to where he stood and snatched the pad from his grasp. I quickly tucked it away in the drawer from his sight.

"I can materialize anywhere." He spoke hardly above a whisper, his face half-smothered in the shadow.

"What?" I felt the screams of frustration at the back of my throat.

"You asked how I can come and go without your notice," he paused. "It's part of the perks of the un-dead." I caught a glimmer of his smile. "I sorta happened into it. Diablo, with his foul sense of humor, thought it'd be funny to throw a lit torch at me. I darted from the flame as it charged at me like a bullet. That's when it happened. Like a puff of smoke, I was gone. I landed in the middle of the Eastwick River twenty miles from the barn."

"You can't keep popping in on me, unannounced." I bit my bottom lip, drinking in his stature. His beauty was intoxicating. It would be easy to lose myself with him.

Then a dark thought crossed my mind. "Can any of the others pop in and out like you?" My heart pounded against my chest.

"I don't know. We don't talk much." The corner of his lips twitched.

I hugged my waist. "What happened to vampires not entering a house until they're invited?"

"Technically, I'm not a vampire." Humor churned in his enchanting voice. "I don't mean to frighten you, but I doubt your dad would like me showing up at your front door."

I scoffed, "No joke." Our eyes locked. "How long have you been watching?" I wished he was like every other normal boy, but that was an impossible wish.

"Not long," he whispered.

"Come sit on the roof with me. I'm sorta grounded. It's nice to have someone to talk to." A smile slipped through my lips.

Valentine appeared aloof. By now, he would've kissed me. My brows pulled together into a frown. Something was wrong.

"Hmm... I can't. I didn't come here to hang out." His lips tightened. "Wendy wants to talk to you." He stepped into the moonlight. "She's waiting at the barn."

Dread poured over me. "Do you know what she wants?" Oh, God! She knew I had discovered her identity, the sire.

"Wendy didn't say, but she's like a hen on a hot tin roof. I left her pacing the floor."

I bit my bottom lip hard. At this point, I had no other alternative but to tell him. "Valentine, I have something to confess, but you're not going to like it."

His face grew dim. "What did you do now?"

I wrinkled my nose. "It's not what I've done. It's what I'm about to do."

"Go on," he urged.

"Candy and I met Wendy yesterday at the park. The plan was for Candy to throw holy water on your girl. If the water burned her skin, I intended to stake the witch and end this fiasco once and for all." I swallowed, grimacing, feeling my sandpapered throat. "But it didn't go as planned. We got caught by the principal before we had a chance."

"Why did you do that when I told you she's not the sire?" His words rushed at me like rocks.

"Valentine," I moistened my chapped lips. "If not Wendy, then who?"

He tipped his head back, glaring at the ceiling, his lips flat with anger. Then he cut his eyes back at me. "Have you lost your mind?"

Ire ripped through me. "No, I haven't. Do you have a better idea? Candy and I have been racking our brains trying to figure this out. I gotta get this thing cleared up. I have other problems in my life to worry about, like my dad marrying the bride of Frankenstein."

"At least you have someone to worry over. When this virus or curse is expelled, you have a home to go to," he pointed to himself. "I become homeless."

My eyes grew round as I realized Valentine's dilemma. "I'm sorry. I didn't take into account how this might affect you." I'd forgotten about Valentine's homelessness. I was so caught up in my own problems that I didn't think about him.

His violet eyes welled. "If getting you out of this hell means my death, so be it. I'm dead already. This would be the one thing I've done right in my entire life. At least I'll rest in peace knowing you're safe."

"Valentine, you're a good person. You deserve happiness too." I reached out and grasped his hand.

"I've been defiant all my life. Countless arrests. I've spent time in juvie more times than I care to count. I never was part of society. I was an outsider as much then as I am now. So, I don't matter. Getting you cured is what matters most. You have a chance in life that I've never had. If anyone should get a second chance, it's you."

"Don't say that! You do matter. To me, you matter and to Candy too." My heart ached for him.

He snarled with a short laugh. "I nearly fed on your friend. I highly doubt that."

I teased. "Well, from afar, maybe."

He laughed, and I smiled.

"We have to go," he urged.

"I guess I'll meet you outside," I said.

"I can carry you with me to where I parked my bike."

"You mean like a magician with his disappearing rabbit?"

"Something like that," he laughed softly.

"I don't get it. If you can materialize to and fro, then why do you need your bike?"

"I've not fully developed my abilities. Since my life is waning, I become weaker. I tire often. The bike gets me around when I'm not up for the occasion. I have to drink blood to gain full access to my abilities. Though I try to deny my urges."

I touched my neck. "I understand. My throat feels like strep throat times a million and one?"

"No matter how bad it gets, you have to resist." His brows dipped into an affronted frown as he stepped closer to me. His cool breath fanned my cheeks.

"I'm not as strong as you." My eyes filled with tears.

"You are stronger than you think." Valentine drew me into his powerful arms and gently kissed me. It was sweet like a kiss on a first date. I looked into his eyes, longingly. If only we could.

He bent his lips to my ear and whispered. "I love you." As he drew me closer into his arms, I wept. For a few seconds, I buried my face into the nook of his shoulder, our bodies melted together as one. I knew with all my heart that I loved him too.

Then my moment of basking came to a quick halt when I thought of Wendy. I pulled from his embrace and nodded, knowing what I must do next. I spun on my feet, calling over my shoulder. "Wait!" I rushed to my closet and pulled out my bookbag and shouldered it. "I have stakes and holy water. I'm not stepping into an ambush. I'd rather be wrong than dead."

Valentine shook his head. "Let's go." He swooped me up into his arms, and in an instant, we were standing in front of his bike.

* * *

227

As we sped down the tree-lined road of Eastwick, I stared up at the moon, thinking it looked like a half-eaten marshmallow. The night air had a crisp bite, and riding on the back of Valentine's bike intensified it.

In moments, we were paving a path through the open field of weeds. I spotted Wendy's convertible, black Mercedes-Benz glinting in the faint moonlight. Beside her car, two Harley bikes. Alarm whipped through me like a typhoon. I called out over Valentine's shoulder, asking, "I thought this was a private meeting."

"You forget. My brothers live here." Valentine came to a halt, parking next to the other line of vehicles.

"Oh, yeah," I inhaled a fretful breath as I slid off the back of the bike. My mind screamed dread. Staking Wendy, with his two blood brothers present, might throw a wrench in my plans. Pain hit my gut, and I suddenly needed to barf.

I had one thing to be grateful for, and that was Candy's absence. Otherwise, this meeting could get ugly. I did regret not having a chance to apologize to him for dragging him into this atrocity. If this turned out to be an ambush, chances were, I wouldn't get the opportunity to tell him. My biggest regret.

With my teeth on edge and my heart in my throat, I padded my way to the barn. Valentine followed closely behind me. As I yanked the door open, it screeched in protest. Entering, Valentine reached out discreetly and tugged at my hand. Knowing he had my back helped my unsettled nerves, but for all I knew, he could be part of the ambush. I exchanged a quick glance with Valentine and made my way over to where Wendy sat on a bale of hay toward the left corner. An overhead light swung low from the twenty-foot vaulted ceiling. Shadows danced about on the boarded walls, giving me shivers down my spine. There was a linger of mildew and hay that favored the atmosphere. I instantly felt a sneeze coming on.

Like a creepy painting on the wall, I spotted Diablo and Romeo quietly sitting beside Wendy. Their eyes stalked my every move. I recalled my last encounter with those two jerks, and a swift burst of anger caught in my chest. I wanted to rip their heads off for hurting Candy. I guess that was my inner vampire.

"What took you so long?" Wendy flew to her feet, hands on her hips, eyes blazing at me.

"Sorry. I'm not in the habit of jumping whenever you bark. I'm here now."

"We have a problem that needs to be resolved." Her stormy eyes narrowed at me.

"What problem?" I figured I'd play dumb and see how much she revealed to me. I dropped my bag to the floor with the flap unfastened. If she decided to attack, I had to be ten steps ahead.

"You weren't lying. Our parents really are planning to marry."

"No, joke!" I scoffed. My fingers were itching for a stake.

"I don't plan to lose my wealth over some squandering lover."

Pinning her glint to mine, I stepped into her personal space. "My dad is not a squanderer."

"I don't care!" Wendy shouted like her tongue was on fire. "Grace promised me that I am the sole beneficiary of her will. I am not about to share that with your father."

"Look! I'm not happy about their marriage either."

"So, let's stop this matrimony from happening," Wendy gritted through her teeth.

"How do you intend to stop them? They're two adults." Talk about a grandiose attitude.

An impish grin grew across her face. "I'm a witch. We have enough here to conjure up a spell." She nodded to Diablo and Romeo.

Diablo pressed out a sleazy grin, gathering himself to his feet. He glided his way to my side, as usual, up to no good. But without a word, Valentine stepped in front of me, blocking him. He stood tall, glaring at Diablo as if daring him to fight. Fear iced my spine. He was no match for his older brother.

Valentine spoke out in a forceful voice. "We made a deal, remember?" His eyes turned cold as steel.

"Whatever you want, little brother. I stand by my word." His lips drew back, revealing fangs, but he stepped away. A sense of relief washed over me as I exhaled a silent breath.

But then alarm seized me as I grabbed Valentine's sleeve in my fists. "What deal?"

Valentine's eyes glided to mine, sorrow burned deeply. "Don't worry. I handled some business for them in exchange that they leave you and your family alone, including your little friend."

"Did you commit a crime?" Worry squeezed my heart.

"Micki, the less you know, the better."

"Why would you risk yourself for me?"

"Isn't it obvious?" he whispered.

I was caught off guard by his admission to offer any objection. Valentine was an ever-changing mystery, and I sensed I'd never fully know him.

Wendy's loud voice erupted. "Can we focus on the purpose of this meeting, please?" She glowered at us and then anchored her baleful eyes on Diablo. "Stop ogling the blonde chick, and let's get this spell cast."

A sudden bout of rage veiled Diablo's face as his long fingers charged for her throat, but he stopped as if he had collided into an invisible wall, slamming his body to the planked floor. An explosion erupted as the floor shook with a billow of thick black smoke and splinters of wood raining down on us.

I had more pressing matters than Diablo's temper-tantrum. I addressed Wendy. "How is some stupid spell going to work?" I didn't believe in magic, but I once didn't believe in vampires either. I was wrong then, and I was probably wrong now.

"Trust me. When we have eight people, the spell will work." Wendy snorted confidence, hands resting on her hips.

"Eight? We have only five." My eyes washed over the headcount.

A self-gratifying grin bedeviled Wendy's lips. "I've taken the liberty of inviting others."

No more than Wendy had boasted, a car door slammed, and three others followed. Footfalls crunched across the pebbles, then the barn door creaked open. Panic scraped the back of my neck as my eyes collided with Candy. His aura, red and inflamed as the white in his eyes flitted.

Then, my eyes deadlocked on the two girls escorting my friend, Wendy's posse Ella, and Cindy. Why was I not surprised? My anger boiled to an all high. Apparently, they forced him to come. I whipped around, teeth bared at Wendy. "Why is Candy here?"

"I said we needed eight heads. Candy makes eight. Besides, your friend is our insurance in case you decide to bail."

I flung my heated scowl at Valentine. "Did you know about this?"

His jaw twitched. He didn't have to say a word. His dark pink aura said it all. "I knew they were bringing him, but Wendy promised he wouldn't get hurt."

I raised my hand and brought it down across his left cheek. The slap hit the air with a loud thump. "You betrayed me!"

Stroking his jaw, his lyrical voice stabbed my heart. "I'm sorry. I didn't have a choice." Remorse laid heavily in his words, but I wasn't totally convinced.

I nodded to Candy. "C'mere." He scrambled to my side and hunkered down behind me. I realized more than ever that Valentine couldn't be trusted. It was up to me to save Candy.

Where was Superman when you needed him?

Candy bent his ear toward me and whispered. "Boo, I woke up in my bed, and those mofo witches were looking at me like they were ready to eat me."

I shook my head at him and squeezed his hand for reassurance. Since Valentine was a Benedict Arnold, it looked like it was just Candy and me. Great! Just freaking great!

Although not all was lost. I had forgotten, vampire blood coursed through my veins too. I could put up a good fight, and with the stakes and holy water stashed in my bag, I might detain them long enough for Candy to escape.

"I have an idea," I spoke out. "Let Candy go. Your posse can return him back to where they found him, and you and I can cast the spell together." If Wendy saw that I had decided to be a willing participant, she might cave and set Candy free. Yet, I worried that Diablo and Romeo would go after Candy.

"It's not that simple. There's another issue I have with you," Wendy announced.

I rolled my eyes. "Good grief! Get in line."

"You think I'm the sire. News flash. I am not."

My mouth dropped open. Valentine ratted me out. The fierceness of my hate blazed like an oven. "You think I'm gonna take your word at face value?" I hurled back.

233

"Are you that stupid?" Wendy laughed. If I were the sire, do you think I'd be chit-chatting with you and these losers?"

"If you're not the sire, then who is?"

She threw her head back and burst into laughter. "Silly girl! Do you think I'm that stupid?"

Complete surprise was etched on Valentine's face. "If you can identify the sire, I think you should."

Diablo spoke up, "Why do you care, little brother? Immorality at your feet and you spit on it." His hostile glare was as hard as marble. "You sicken me."

Valentine answered in a cool, collected voice, but underneath, I sensed his anger near the brink of exploding. "Some things far exceed the cost."

Without warning, Romeo sprung to his feet. There was a cruelty about his eyes and mouth that betrayed him for the bloodsucker he was.

Valentine ignored Romeo and pointed his angry eyes at Diablo.

"Brother, you have betrayed us." Diablo's lips curled back in hatred as if he couldn't deny himself the pleasure of revealing the razor-sharp canines.

"This is no gift!" Valentine lashed out. "An eternal life robbing innocent humans of *their* lives? What right do we have to make that call?" Violent static electricity hummed in the air from the intensity in Valentine's stiff body. I feared for the inevitable. I clung to Candy, watching in silence.

Wendy nodded to Romeo. "Take the skinny boy and hold him until I say differently."

I sprang into action, grabbing a stake from my bag and aimed it at Wendy's chest and then at Romeo. "Don't touch him!" I bit down on the pain as the stench of burning skin assaulted my nostrils.

I'd forgotten about the two girls when Cindy's high-pitched voice pierced the air. "Uh... Wendy, you promised us no trouble. You all can handle your own family squabble. This has nothing to do with Ella and me."

Shock rippled through me. I never thought they had enough tenacity to deny her of anything. *Way to go, girls!* I watched as they strutted to the door. My eyes cut to Wendy. Beads of sweat dotted her forehead.

Valentine's gentle hand touched my shoulder as he stepped in front of both Candy and me. "I'm afraid I'm with Micki on this one." He pointed his deadly eyes at Romeo. "Stay back if you want to live."

A blood-red smile crossed Romeo's lips, revealing ivory fangs and endless hunger. Still, it didn't stop Valentine. In a flash, the two were facing off, crouched, circling each other, both baring teeth and growling like two furious lions.

It was apparent that Romeo's continuous feeding had given him savage strength that far surpassed Valentine's abilities.

My heart was in my throat as I feared for my friend.

In a cat's eye, Romeo and Valentine charged, colliding into each other, bones cracking, blood splattering like buckets of red paint. Death scented the air.

Valentine's limp body went flying like a rocket, smacking into a high beam, and snapping in two. Down his body dropped twenty feet, hitting the plank floor with a renowned thump. The floor shook like an earthquake.

I staggered to my feet, shooting to Valentine's side as he lay still with no signs of life, but Diablo caught me, stopping me in my tracks. He banded his arm around my neck, holding me tight against his body. I struggled to free myself, though his strength overpowered mine. He pressed his lips to my hair and whispered. "Watch your boyfriend die. And then, your little human friend is next."

"I swear!" I swallowed the tears wedged in my throat. "If you kill them, I won't rest until you're staked!" I sputtered with rage.

Diablo roared with laughter. "Too late, my sweet."

I jerked my arms to break his grip but to no avail. I was helpless and forced to watch my friend die.

Romeo stalked over to Valentine's limp body, snatching him up and hurling him like a feathered pillow. Valentine's limp body flew through the roof, boards snapping and crashing to the floor.

Then everything stilled, and death hovered in silence. Only the relentless tapping of blood dripping from the rafters echoed. Yet no sign of Valentine.

Loss gripped my stomach as reality struck. Valentine was dead. Gone forever.

Now Romeo pinned his attention to the only human in the room. A startled whimper rose from

Candy. Standing helpless and alone, his shoulders shook.

Oh, my God! I swiftly turned to Diablo. "*Please, don't hurt him.*"

"Why is the human so important to you?" he asked. "In a few short weeks, the boy will be nothing more than a snack." Diablo's fangs nipped dangerously at my neck.

A sudden bout of curdling screams came from Wendy, startling everyone's attention. "How stupid can you be? You promised me no bloodshed." Her baleful eyes darted between Diablo and Romeo. "You weren't supposed to hurt Valentine!" Spittle flew from her mouth. "I love him!" Wendy twirled on her feet, arms spread wide, face red and twisted with unprecedented rage. "I curse you to the hell you belong!"

Gasps curled the air as all eyes fell on Valentine. He was standing in front of Candy, blocking Romeo from further harm.

"He's alive," I murmured, yet I sensed something different. His eyes, his demeanor, all held a sense of *predatory nature.*

I could do nothing but watch, frozen in place as Romeo charged Valentine, but the battle had shifted. Romeo swung the first blow but missed. Valentine ducked and delivered a mind-boggling left jab, clipping Romeo under his chin. He took flight ramming his heart through a pitchfork. The fork's teeth protruded from his blood-covered chest. The smell of decay spread throughout the barn, the scent of vampire blood. I studied Romeo's limp body. Shock colored his face as he took his last breath. His eyes went glossed over and went stiff.

When I thought the fight had run its course, terror caught my breath once more. I spotted blood dripping from the corner of Valentine's mouth, but the blood wasn't his. My eyes rounded as I gasped in horror. Oh no! Valentine had ... *crossed.* "No! No! No!" I ranted, tears flooding my vision. "Not Valentine!" *But it made sense.* His surprising strength! Though when could he have fed and whose human life did he take?

God, if only I'd not involved him. This was my fault. All mine! He was protecting Candy and me, but this wasn't in the plan. He was supposed to live! All my strength vanished, and my legs buckled under me. Diablo released his steel grip, letting me fall to the floor with a heavy clonk.

Wendy came to my side and screeched at Diablo. "Get away from her!" She hissed through her teeth. "Monsters! You and Romeo. Freakin' animals!"

Diablo reached his long fingers for Wendy's throat but halted when a familiar voice pierced the chill.

"My goodness. What a mess you children have made." Her soft, musical voice purred.

All eyes froze on the unexpected visitor. I gasped, running to Candy's side. He threw his arms around me, trembling. I whispered, half to myself, "What the hell!"

My eyes slid to Valentine. Tall and majestic, he knuckled the blood from the corner of his mouth, unfazed by the intruder. His appearance seemed larger, his eyes darker and sharper... a look of a vicious hunter. He glanced back at me; sorrow churned in his eyes. I saw his aura, indigo... *regret.*

Wendy's startled eyes fixed on the visitor broke the silence, "Mom, what are you doing here?"

Grace glided her way over to her daughter and smiled, touching her cheek lovingly. Though, I didn't sense anything mothering about her gesture. "I could hear you from the road," she claimed. "I thought I should drop in and see what all the commotion is about."

Wendy's brows furrowed. "We're fine."

"I can see that." Her eyes roamed over the barn, soaking in the upheaval from the ceiling to the floor and then halting on Romeo's bloody body.

Wendy shook her head; confusion veiled her fair face. "Mother, you should leave."

"You're foolish to think that I don't know about your vampire friends?" A storm of sinister intent rolled off her tongue. "They are my creation. All of them, my darling."

Sudden shock slammed into my chest. It was Grace all this time. "Oh, my God!" Fear muffled my scream. "You're the *sire,* but... but Wendy's your daughter, a human. How is that possible?"

Valentine's stature went ridged. Though not a word did he utter, his hungry eyes never left Grace.

Grace faced me. The cold light of evil shone in her eyes. "Why do you make assumptions?" One corner of her lip twitched. "Wendy is adopted."

"What?" Wendy laughed at Grace. "Mother, tell them the truth."

"Yes, darling. I'm afraid they are right. I saw your gifts. I knew then you'd be such an asset to my collection," Grace admitted.

"Stop kidding around, Mother. You're scaring me," Wendy's voice appeared strained.

"Yes," Grace answered. "Magic runs deep in your veins. Your parents were gifted as well."

"My parents?" Wendy faintly echoed Grace's words.

"Darling, they're no longer with us, I'm afraid."

"They're dead?" Wendy whispered, stunned.

"Yes." Grace's eyes gleamed. "Taking their lives was for the greater good."

Wendy's face paled. "You... you killed my real parents. Why?"

"They would've never appreciated your abilities as I do."

"So, you took their lives because..." she stammered, clenching her chest.

Grace's well-manicured brows furrowed. "My actions were justified, darling. Like I do everything else, I did it for the higher power."

I intervened, anger clawing down my spine. "It's not okay to hurt others for your own selfish gain, Grace!" Unequivocally, I hated her.

Grace snapped her head up at me and snarled through her sharp teeth. "Must your judgment be so harsh? I did her a wonderful favor. Wendy's parents would have prevented her from reaching her full potential. A blood-witch."

I had to make sense of this insanity. "Why my father? What does he have that grabs your interest?"

Grace's pomposity oozed from her whole demeanor. "You wouldn't cross!" she paused. "If you had only taken your first kill, I would've never involved your father. It was you I desired."

"Why me?"

"My dear, you're reading my aura now. You are quite talented. You and Wendy have a common interest. You both are bestowed with a special gift. You'd be of great service to me."

"I guess we'll never know because I'm not joining your coven, Grace," I refuted.

"I think your father has served his purpose." Grace flashed a baleful smile as Henry appeared, standing beside her. It was as if he'd been dropped from the sky. He just suddenly materialized.

The toxin of terror blazed through me as this nightmare deepened. Henry stood there, nothing more than a statue, staring blankly off into space.

Grace's smooth voice jarred my eyes back to her. "Valentine, come. You must drink his blood to replenish your strength. My blood will soon burn through your veins. Come… *drink, darling!*" she cooed, holding Henry's shoulders, tugging back his collar, exposing the jugular vein.

Valentine's face churned with dark thirst. He licked his lips as if his mouth throbbed for the urgent need of his fangs to feed. His predatory glint was nailed to my dad as he edged slowly toward him.

"No!" I pleaded. "Valentine, don't!"

I didn't recognize my friend at all. His boyish features had hardened. The sweetness in his eyes had vanished and, in its place, came malice.

"Yes, Sire," Valentine's voice was soft as satin and yet, vile as the devil.

"Valentine, please!" I started to rush to Henry's side, but as if my feet were cemented to the floor, I couldn't move. No matter how hard I tried to lift my feet, I was stuck, frozen in place.

"Oh, you poor, poor child. You're too pigheaded to see the benefits," Grace laughed. "It's simple, child. Cross and your father will go unharmed."

"I'll cross, Grace! First, let my dad and Candy go unharmed. I'll do whatever you want but leave them out of this monstrosity," I begged.

"Your mortal mind has blinded you. Once you cross, you shall live without any bounds." Grace believed in the lie, but I didn't. I never would.

"No limits, huh? You call never walking in daylight freedom?" I countered.

One corner of her lip twitched, detest cavorted in her iniquitous eyes. "The sun seems to be such a trivial thing when you can have the world at your feet?" Her reasoning had gone past the moon, making no sense.

"Let's get this over with," I bit out.

"Very well." Grace flashed a cherry-red smile. "Give me your wrist," she ordered.

242

Candy grabbed my arm in haste. "No, gul! Don't give in to her." His hand trembled against my skin. I smiled into his caramel face. So sweet and close to my heart. "Candy, I will love you forever." I laid my hand against his cheek and locked his eyes with mine. "Watch over my family, will you?" I turned from him as a tear fell from my cheek. Candy's sobbing drifted to my ears. What choice did I have? My life or theirs.

I refused to give her the satisfaction of seeing me cower. So, I met her eyes as equally as I tilted my chin and straightened my shoulders back, I made my way to Grace's side, my wrist extended for her to take. Her cherry lips curled back, exposing the sharp canines she had kept hidden until now. She sickened me as I saw the thirst in her eyes that made her quiver with anticipation. I wanted to vomit. I never hated someone more than I hated her at this moment.

Then everything spun out of control so fast that I didn't realize what had happened until it was all over. First, it sounded like the sky falling all around us. A huge crash tore through the side of the barn. Boards and beams from the roof crashed around us. Valentine tackled both Candy and me, knocking us out of the way of the fatal collapse. A screeching voice slammed into the air. I looked up, staring into terror. Grandpa's El Camino plowed into Grace, knocking her under the wheel. The truck bounced off her mangled body.

Before I could knock the sense back into my brain, Valentine grabbed up a stake and pierced Grace's body, ramming the stake through her heart. Blood showered her broken body like crimson rain.

My gaze rolled over Candy as he lay still, unconscious on the floor and covered in debris. I dropped to my knees and shook his shoulders furiously. Tears streamed down my face. But then his eyes opened, and he bounced back to life as his eyes bugged. "What happened?" he mumbled, half sitting up.

I threw my arms around his neck and held him tight to me. "Oh, thank God! You're okay," I sobbed.

"Yeah, I think all my parts are still workin'." He rubbed his head and patted his chest. "Are you, okay?"

"I'm good." I used my sleeve to wipe the tears from my face. My attention went to Valentine. I rose to my feet and ran to his side, but I came to an abrupt halt. Terror ripped through me once more. The only thing left in his place was his clothes smothered underneath ashes. *His ashes.* I dropped to my knees, wailing. Candy came to my side and scooped me up into his arms. "He took his life to save us, Candy." I choked through tears. "He knew crossing and staking the sire would end his life, but he took Grace's life anyway." I wiped the tears from my face and combed my eyes over the barn.

First, I spotted Romeo's ashes underneath the pitchfork and Diablo, nothing left but a pile of dirty clothes mixed with black soot.

Wendy stood alone, pulling at her hair. By the stark expression on her face, she was in shock. Then my eyes landed on Henry. He was blinking as if he were waking up from a dream. He was safe, unharmed, and I knew I'd have a lot of explaining to do.

Then my eyes landed on Grandpa. He was slowly creeping out of his crashed car. He suffered a few minor cuts here and there, but he appeared to be in good shape. The El Camino was totally demolished. But that was the least of our troubles. I leaped to my feet and ran to Grandpa, throwing my arms around him. "Are you hurt? How did you know?"

"Aye, Lassie, I'm grand." He tossed me a weak smile. "Doesn't everyone know that this town is full of damn vampires?" he grumbled, hugging me back. "How 'bout we pack our stuff up and move to California? A beach house maybe. Warm weather and lots of sunshine," he mumbled to himself as he staggered outside the barn.

Candy and Wendy stood beside my dazed dad as I ran to him. "Dad!" I cried. "Are you hurt?"

"I'm fine. I think." Confusion enshrouded his pale face. "What... what happened?" His glossed eyes ran over the barn. "It looks like a war zone in here." Apart from shock, Henry appeared in good shape, and relief swirled inside me.

My eyes then focused on Wendy. Her shoulders were slumped and trembling from weeping. I came to her side and threw my arm over her shoulder. "You can come home with us tonight. You shouldn't be alone." I smiled, watching her frail body tremble.

She wiped her tears with the back of her sleeve and said, "I didn't know."

"Wendy, everything is in the past."

Her brows crinkled, "I'm sorry for every vile thing I've ever done to you. I don't know why I did it, and I had no idea my mother was a ..." she choked out.

"None of us knew she was a vampire. And I don't think you were yourself. It seems that Grace had you under some sort of spell. Come on," I gently nudged. "How about some soup? My dad makes the best chicken soup in the whole wide world." I laughed to myself. My appetite had returned, and I was starving.

# Creatures of the Night

Months passed since that gruesome night. We never spoke of it either. It was as if it never happened. I think if we talked about what went down, we'd have to accept that vile creatures of the night existed. I was a believer.

My mother, Joan, finally left Phil and asked me to move back with her to New York. I kindly declined her offer and explained that I preferred to live with Dad and Grandpa. She was hurt at first, but after a while, she adapted to her new single life. Mom finally got her happily ever after.

As for the Eastwick estate, Grace vanished from thin air. Eastwick Manor up the hill on the old Eastwick Road fell apart overnight. The old manor couldn't hold its luster any longer, and like its master, it lost its glory and fame. The city ordinance declared it condemned. The only thing left to give proof of Grace's existence was the Eastwick barn. Despite its condition, the Historic Preservation Commission deemed it as a historical marker. The city fenced it off and posted a *No Trespassing sign*.

Wendy's biological uncle, Mike, her father's brother, stepped forward. It emerged that Mike had been searching for Wendy since her abduction at birth. Grace lied about the adoption. Though, she didn't lie about murdering the parents. Grace stole Wendy after she'd killed her parents, James, and Kara Belle. Last I heard, Wendy was doing well, returning to her true roots. She put away her magic wand and began horseback riding.

As for the two girls that clung to Wendy's skirt, Ella and Cindy, they disappeared, and no one had seen them since. And strangely, no one seemed concerned. It was as if they never existed.

Henry didn't remember much about Grace. It was as if she was a faint dream. I think it was safe to assume that he'd been under the influence of a vampire's trance. That was a mystery that would never come to full circle. After a while, Henry started dating, but no one special just yet.

Grandpa was still busy as ever, and he and Henry were making more time for fishing. Some things never change. I still refused to dig up worms and continued to get ribbed for my stance.

Candy and I were close as ever. We attended Eastwick Community College. We plan to get a degree in journalism and start a paranormal investigation company traveling the world.

I often wondered about Valentine. He was my first crush and the first boy I'd kissed. I thought I loved him. And I did. I always would. I couldn't speak about his whereabouts. Unlike the others, his ashes had disappeared. Vanished from thin air, much like he often did.

One time, Candy and I went to a Christmas event downtown. Eastwick, every year for the holidays, decorated the downtown. Horses and buggies, music blasting Christmas carols, food service, and an outdoor ice-skating rink. Candy, not the best skater, clung to me like glue. But we laughed and giggled, being just two teenagers.

One unsuspecting evening, my eyes drifted to the foliage past the tree line, and I caught a quick glimpse of someone in the shadows, watching. I gasped, wondering if it was *him*. But then, the silhouette vanished as quickly as I had spotted it. Chills covered my body. Perhaps my mind was toying with me.

Grace was destroyed. And everything with her died. But if Valentine somehow survived, I hoped he'd found happiness. Vampire or not, in the end, he saved my family and me. Weirdly, he was my Superman.

Dear reader,

We hope you enjoyed reading *The Crossing*. Please take a moment to leave a review, even if it's a short one. Your opinion is important to us.

Discover more books by Jo Wilde at https://www.nextchapter.pub/authors/jo-wilde

Want to know when one of our books are free or discounted? Join the newsletter at http://eepurl.com/bqqB3H

Best regards,
Jo Wilde and the Next Chapter Team

The story continues in:

The Haunting

To read the first chapter for free, please head to:
https://www.nextchapter.pub/books/the-haunting

The Crossing
ISBN: 978-4-86750-618-9 (Mass Market)

Published by
Next Chapter
1-60-20 Minami-Otsuka
170-0005 Toshima-Ku, Tokyo
+818035793528
10th June 2021